Aveline couldn't tear her eyes away. The man was gorgeous—and most unfriendly…

One of the men stood out from the others. His clothing was obviously expensive, despite its poor condition. Aveline stood quietly and observed him through the crack of the door, wondering who he was.

He discarded his brown swallowtail coat and threw it over the stall wall, leaving only a green cotton waistcoat and a worn, white linen shirt covering his upper torso. The shirt hung open, exposing the man's broad chest, dusted with dark hair. The waistcoat, also unbuttoned, trailed down toward brown corduroy trousers that fit snugly around his muscled thighs. His clothes were unmarked by patches, though stains from dirt surrounded both knees. He wore brown stockings with black leather brogues.

She wanted to stand in the doorway and watch him sing for the rest of the day. His voice was wonderful and its warm tone washed through her. But she knew the longer she remained the more likely it was she'd be seen. As an eavesdropper, she had seen and learned more information than her father would ever have allowed. That is why she loved doing it.

The time grew late and she decided to leave. She'd introduce herself when she wouldn't be an interruption. Her success on the farm revolved around their good opinion of her. Easing away, she stumbled and grabbed a hold of the door, causing it to creak. Suddenly, the Irishman looked directly at her. The grin she'd seen on his face just moments before turned to a scowl.

She did not stick around to see what he did next, but ran in the direction of the farmhouse. He caught her arm in three quick strides, grabbed her wrist, and spoke to her in Gaelic as she turned around, gasping for breath. His language was beautiful. She just wished she understood what he was trying to say.

She is left with an offer she cannot refuse...

Upon his death in 1823, English nobleman, Lord Peyton leaves his daughter Lady Aveline with two choices—stay single and inherit only a small farm in Ireland, where she might just be able to eke out a living, or get married and live in luxury, inheriting all his wealth and property. Fiercely independent, Aveline heads for Ireland only to run afoul of her father's farm manager, the devastatingly handsome Ciaran O'Devlin. Alone in a strange country, Aveline yearns for love and friendship, but Ciaran offers only criticism and disdain. Confused and angered by strange visions and her growing attraction to Ciaran, Aveline is determined to make the farm prosper—despite the insufferable Irishman.

He has a secret he cannot reveal...

Ciaran mistrusts Aveline's intentions and refuses to admit that a willful, *English* woman now owns the farm that should have been his. Although he insists Aveline should go back to England, he cannot deny their budding passion. Yet, he knows—even if she doesn't—that nothing can come of it. Not only can't a poor Irishman marry an English noblewoman, but when Aveline learns of his past, she'll want nothing more to do with him. Ciaran has always known that each decision carries a consequence, but it's only when he stands to lose Aveline that he realizes what a heavy price his past decisions may have.

KUDOS for *To Love an Irishman*

To Love an Irishman by Diva Jefferson is a classic historical romance. Set in both England and Ireland, the story revolves around an English aristocrat, Lady Aveline Peyton, and a poor Irish farmer, Ciaran O'Devlin, who is the manager of the small Irish farm belonging to Lord Peyton, Aveline's father. When Lord Peyton dies, he gives Aveline quite a shock. Although she expected him to die, being as he was ill, she hadn't expected him to try to force her into marriage through the terms of his will. According to that will, if Aveline gets married, she inherits everything. However, if she stays single, she inherits only a small farm in Ireland, where she just might be able to survive—if she's lucky...The plot of *To Love an Irishman* has a few surprises along the way, including a charming little ghost and a kidnapping—things that kept my interest keen. So grab a hot cup of tea, settle down by the fire, and enjoy! – *Taylor Jones, Reviewer*

To Love an Irishman by Diva Jefferson is a classic historical romance. But classic doesn't mean it's boring. Not in the least. If fact, Jefferson soups up her story with a touch of the paranormal—a vision of a child to come—some danger in the form of a villain who wants revenge on Ciaran and takes it out on Aveline, and some sweet and frustrating romance. The book has the flavor of Ireland as well as a feeling of authenticity, heightened by Jefferson's use of a number of Gaelic words, which might be intimidating if she hadn't also included a glossary. Which I thought was a brilliant touch...The storyline is strong, and the plot had some nice surprises...All in all, I quite enjoyed *To Love an Irishman*. – *Regan Murphy, Reviewer*

To Love an

Irishman

Large Print

DIVA JEFFERSON

A Black Opal Books Publication

GENRE: HISTORICAL ROMANCE/ PA-
RANORMAL

This is a work of fiction. Names, places,
characters and incidents are either the prod-
uct of the author's imagination or are used
fictitiously, and any resemblance to any ac-
tual persons, living or dead, businesses, or-
ganizations, events or locales is entirely co-
incidental.

TO LOVE AN IRISHMAN ~ Large Print
Copyright © 2011 by Diva Jefferson
Cover Design by NePaul Wilson
All cover art copyright © 2012
All Rights Reserved
Large Print ISBN: 978-1-626942-62-2

First Publication: MARCH 2012

DEDICATION

To my love, Connor,
whom I would be lost without.

Irish-English Glossary with Pronunciation

an fear (un far) – the man

Ba mhaith liom luí leat (bah hwah lyum loo lyat) – I would like to make love with you.

bagtard (bag-tar'd) – expletive for angry frustration

blather (bla-thur) – your talk

Bodhrán agus Bones (bōr-AHn ahguhs bōns) – Bodhrán and Bones (Irish frame drum)

cailín (kah-leen) - girl

ceilí (kay-lee) – Irish band

colleen (kah-leen) – girl

craic (krak) - fun

dathúil (dah-HOO-il) – beautiful

Éire (Air-ah) – Ireland

Éireannach uisce beatha (AY-ron-ock ish-ga ba-ha) – Irish whiskey

Fáilte go Néamh (Fowl-cha gō Nahv) – Welcome to Heaven.

fla (flâ) – to copulate

Gaelic (Gaelik) – Irish language

Gráim thú (Graw-eem hoo) – I love you.

inis (in-nish) – island

mo ghrá (mô graw) – my love

mo iníon (mô ih-NEE-in) – my daughter

ní (nee-HA) – no

ní me (nee-HA may) – not me

och (ôck) – but, oh
port (pohrt) – Irish jig
punts (puhnts) – Irish currency, pounds
Sasanach or *Sassenach* (sass-en-nack) – derogatory term for "Englishman"
Tá tú diaibhlín (Tah too JOWL-een) – You are an imp.
Tabhair póg dom (TOO-irr pogue dum) – Kiss me.
Uilleann (ilen) – Irish pipes
wee (wee) – small

Chapter 1

County Cumbria, England, 1823:

Aveline hoped her father didn't notice her eavesdropping. Through a crack in the door, she watched him tell the solicitor everything he wished to have written into his will. Silver-blue satin curtains surrounded the bed and were swept open to allow light from a single window to shine upon his ashen face. Unfortunately, the sun's hopeful rays could not prevent the rainstorm churning inside her.

The voices were unintelligible from where she stood, and all she could discern from the ramblings was her name. Surely, she was not going deaf? Maybe he lowered his voice on purpose to prevent her hearing. Of course, her father knew how much she liked to nose round. Perhaps he thought the only way to keep her from listening was to whisper.

No. He'd never keep important information from her. He loved her. His current actions must be a precaution in case she napped in the adjoining bedchamber.

She wondered why he'd asked her to leave his room in the first place. Why did he feel the need to spend even fifteen minutes without her when so little time was left?

Before she could answer the question, her father signed the paper on a wooden, bedside table with a shaky hand. He gave the solicitor a smug smile, and Aveline could now hear every word he said. "Please make sure she arrives there, where she will be happy. Tell her I love her."

I will be happy to live in another place? Fifteen minutes is long enough to go mad after all.

"I love you too, papa," she whispered as her eyes welled with tears.

Aveline could not believe the words were her father's final wishes.

The wiry solicitor took the sheet as he lowered his spectacles, "I will return to the manse on the morrow to relay the will to Lady Aveline. A small memorial will be given in your name four days hence. I will not forget the words. May you forever rest in peace after death, my friend. Good day to you, Sir." He rose and headed for the door.

She rushed into her bedroom, and softly shut the door with a trembling hand before the man saw her.

Her father had said he'd fetch her after

he'd talked to the solicitor. Why hadn't he done so yet? Unable to come to terms with the circumstances, she crossed to the bed, laying sideways atop the feathered coverlet, and cried.

Sleep came with great difficulty.

The child was beautiful.

Her mother was proud. Her father was proud. They sat together on the field watching her. She ran upon heather without a care in the world. A smile played on her lips, one curved to the right of her mouth. She beckoned for her parents to follow. They shook their heads, pointing toward the sun. The time had come for supper and they needed to return home for the night.

The little girl's dress was white, and swayed in the breeze. She was tangible enough to touch. She was almost real.

4

👑 👑 👑

A small knock awoke Aveline from the dream. How long had she been asleep?

Her maid never waited to relay news. "Lady Aveline, it's your father…"

Aveline ran into her father's room to find him already gone. Tears filled her eyes and flowed down her cheeks in rivulets. Her father had wanted to die alone, but at least he had been happy at the end. The last expression on his face was a smile. She kissed his forehead and closed his eyelids. His head was turned toward the window and she wondered if the last image he had seen was the green expanse of land surrounding the manse.

She sat next to his bed with her head in her hands. Three hours later, men removed the body, feet first.

In the morning, the solicitor, who introduced himself as Mr. Stowe, notified the local rector, and arranged for a casket to be fashioned. Her mother had been buried in a small graveyard located within the estate grounds and so her father would lie there, too.

👑 👑 👑

Aveline spent the next two days in solitude. She refused to eat or drink and remained in her room. She was a score and one years old, with no husband or family still alive. There was no male heir to pass her father's title to, which meant the earldom would become extinct.

She'd lead a writer's life, a life of spinsterhood, but her future could be fruitful. At least, she certainly hoped so. She fought the tears flowing down her cheeks. She needed to remain strong in order to take hold of her future and make her own way in a world where marriage was considered the only way for a woman to live comfortably.

Her father must have left her a nice sum in his will. She'd get one of her books published with the money. Of course, now that she was an heiress, she could imagine all the suitors would be flocking to her doorstep for the chance at the riches that came with marriage to her. That thought scared her more than anything else. She had always considered herself desirable. Handsome suitors requested dances with her all the time because she was the daughter of an earl.

Now that her father was gone, there would no longer be an Earl of Kendal in her family. The sobs came and she couldn't prevent the flood. A single handkerchief wouldn't protect her clothing from the stream. Her father had always been her protector. Without him around, she didn't know what to do.

Then she remembered about Mills Publishing. Her father had mentioned the place one day and suggested she sell her first novel to them. Well, there was nothing to stop her from becoming a writer and having her novels published now.

Then another thought struck her.

What if her father had entirely different plans for her life that she was not privy to? She groaned. *Did my father encourage me to reject a suitor all those times because he had set me into an arranged marriage with a French viscount or a Spanish prince? I did not hear where he wanted the solicitor to send me, but* there *is most certainly not* here. *Oh no,* her inner voice declared, *this will not do, I do not wish to move from England at all.*

👑 👑 👑

After the memorial, Aveline sat upon a settee in the drawing room. The solicitor, Mr. Stowe, a thin man with a head of salt and pepper hair, did not speak much, nor did he waste time fumbling around in his satchel. The papers and an ink pen were already in his hand. She watched as he applied his rounded spectacles to his nose. Then taking up the folded document with her father's familiar signature, he read the contents of the will in a clear voice.

She felt her breath cease altogether as she heard her fortune relayed to her in her father's words. The thought of him had her eyes welling with tears once again.

She suddenly jerked upright in her sofa as she focused on what the solicitor was saying.

"...second, after the payment of my debts, and funeral expenses, the rest of the money shall be kept by my daughter Aveline Peyton for her use the rest of her life, as well as her heirs thereafter..."

She sighed.

"...fourth, I give to my daughter Lady Aveline Peyton the family estate, as well as the land around..." Those words were exactly what she wished to hear.

He took a deep breath. "...to receive the funds and the property in England on the day of her marriage and not one hour before. Until then, the estate will be kept in trust for her."

What? She'd nowhere to live? She couldn't have heard correctly.

The solicitor faltered. "The...the land owned by me in Altmore, County Tyrone, Ireland is the sole property of Lady Aveline Peyton with or without a marriage union...also she must not—under any circumstances—be accompanied to her destination."

Aveline jumped to her feet. "This is insufferable! I will not be shipped off alone to some—some farm in Ireland."

Is this what he meant when he said I would be happy over there? He wants me to go to Ireland?

The solicitor stared at her.

She slumped back into the chair, wishing he would be done with the will. "Carry on," she growled. "I have a desire to hear what else my father refrained from telling me when he was alive."

Mr. Stowe took off his spectacles and watched her reaction. "That is all of it, my lady."

Aveline knew her mother had been Irish and had met her father when he had visited that country for business purposes, as he often did.

What was she going to do? She was not entitled to any of the funds from the estate until she married. There would hardly be any money left over from her father's bills and funeral expenses. Certainly not enough for her to live comfortably.

No. She refused to believe this. She'd never wanted to marry before, due to the fact she had felt she would be courted for her money. But in order to have the money to get her books published, she might have to do so.

She tried to assess the situation more to her advantage. "Well, it seems the only choice I have left is to leave the country."

Although, she knew any sensible woman would immediately seek a husband and live happily in luxury, she had no choice but to agree with the terms of her father's will. She needed a more fulfilling life that contained less loneliness, one more rich with friendship and ambient laughter, than an arranged marriage would likely give her. She dreamed of becoming a published author, not some man's wife.

"Your father stated the servants shall remain on the estate while it is in trust. They will be paid their regular wages until you return either married or able to afford a year's worth of payment. Do you have any ideas in that regard?" he asked.

Feeling as if she were in a very bad dream, she wrung the black gloves in her hands and tried to prevent another flow of tears from clouding her vision. "Why do you ask? I appear to have no choice in the matter as it is. The farm is the only means of a living for me until I marry. *If* I am ever to marry at all."

"Perhaps you might change your mind someday. Very well, Lady Aveline, then pack your things and make ready to leave." Mr. Stowe started toward the door, but turned in mid-step. "Oh, beg pardon, but I forgot to mention your father wanted me to tell you he loved you."

Aveline refused to look at him. "Yes, I know he did."

He cleared his throat. "A travel carriage will arrive at half past seven tomorrow morning. From here, you will travel to Ravenglass Harbor where the packet ship *Cromwell* is docked. The vessel will take you to Ireland. I would not advise a late arrival, because no more departures are scheduled until next week." He hesitated as if waiting for her to respond, but she had no desire to speak." He cleared his throat again. "Good day to you, then."

Aveline rose, gave him a slight curtsy, and nodded as he walked through the doorway. She watched through the window as he entered the waiting carriage and drove out of sight.

"Damn it all!" she muttered, since no one remained to berate her for her language.

From what she knew of the Irish, they were haughty and stubborn, not to mention thieves and beggars of the worst kind. Or so she learned from Miss McCork, the governess her father had brought into the house. When Aveline would ask her about the people there, the woman told her only of the men. "They are like drunken mules that are unable to stand without ale ravaging their systems." She was judgmental and condescending toward her people, but around Aveline's father she behaved like a true matron of kindness. Aveline had come to the conclusion the woman was only interested in her father for his money.

Now Aveline owned a farm in Ireland. *Why a farm?* The place must be in the middle of nowhere, which meant no friends or suitors for her to entertain. Surely, the farmers could not have the luxuries she took for granted at her father's estate. Endless amounts of paper and ink—and a fine desk for writing.

Although she had found some humor in the governess's prejudices, Aveline knew even though Miss McCork wanted her to look at all the bad, there was probably some good in Ireland, too. After all, her father was not dim-witted. He had written her fate onto a sheet of paper before he passed away. Would he have done so without taking at least some of her needs and desires into consideration?

She ran up the wooden staircase of the manse to pack a trunk of clothes and other necessary items to take with her. They would have to last her a while, to be sure. She spent her last night on English soil, packing for a new life in a place she'd never known, wishing her father was more than just a memory in her heart.

Chapter 2

Waiting at her doorstep for the carriage the next morning, Aveline decided that she was going to learn the real truth about her heritage, about her mother's people. Mrs. Abernathy stood beside her, weeping. She told the maid her father's will stated she was to travel alone and that she sought to comply with his wishes. Obviously distressed to see her unhappy and without any other options, Miss Abernathy had finally agreed to remain behind. When the carriage arrived, Aveline bid farewell to her servants, people she'd known all her life.

The long and gloomy ride took her from the wrought iron gates of her father's estate to Ravenglass on the coast. Miles of grassy-hilled terrain passed her window. She remembered the time she rode her horse over the stonewall that separated her father's estate and lands from the neighbor's. She had been proud to accomplish such a feat on her own, but her father had chastised her for trespassing onto the land of a recluse who resided in his manse with ten large dogs. The dogs had only ceased barking at her when their owner stormed outside to see what the ruckus was about.

Wherever Aveline went, she knew her father's memory would follow her. Yes, she'd miss the townspeople and all the friends she'd met at parties, but she was not particularly close to anyone but her father.

When she arrived at the dock, the hired driver helped her out of the carriage. A blast of sea air collided with her. Its salty smell filled her nostrils. The cool breeze provided relief from the sun's heated rays, if only for the breadth of a minute.

She looked out toward the ocean. The din of the crashing waves was nearly drowned out by the commotion occurring around the ship. She knew her destiny resided beyond the Irish Sea. Did something magnificent await her arrival? Or was that only wishful thinking?

She smiled as the captain, who introduced himself as Captain McAfee, greeted her and led her aboard the broad, three-masted ship. As she walked toward her stateroom on the top deck, an apparition of a little girl in a white dress looked down from the lookout perch. Aveline blinked and the vision was gone.

I must be overtired, she thought as she

walked into the room that was to be her cabin and saw the thick mattress, feather-down duvet, and fluffy cushions. Sleep came soon after she laid her head down on her pillow.

A voice called her name from a distance. Aveline woke. She left the comfort of her room and stepped out into the cool night. The churning seawater growled as the boat separated it with its girth and speed. The temperature had dropped, causing her to shiver. The cold air permeated her gown's thin material. She glanced upward. The apparition stood in the lookout again. The girl's white form remained in the same spot as earlier.

"Who are you?" Aveline whispered into the darkness.

No answer came.

"Are you in need of any assistance? Tell me what I can do to help you."

The girl laughed then disappeared.

That is when Aveline knew the ship had reached Ireland's shores.

County Tyrone, Ireland, 1823:

Aveline arrived in Altmore after a two-day coach ride from the docks. She had felt as if she was the only human being left on Earth as she traveled in a four-in-hand, with six other tourists, along a dirt road through an unfamiliar land. The scenery was awe-inspiring. It spread through a vast landscape containing little or no development. The terrain looked as if it had been untouched by human hands for thousands of years.

An expanse of mountains towered in the distance, reminding her of a time ten years ago when a younger version of herself had stood at the edge of a cliff pretending, with arms outstretched, to be the queen of everything. Her father had come up behind her, his voice filled with amusement. "This day is blessed with the arrival of Queen Aveline. All hail the queen!"

"Silly papa, I am not a queen. I am the ruler of the world." As she turned back around, her foot caught a rock that stuck out near the edge. "Oh no!"

Her father caught her arm just in time to keep her from falling.

"I will not let the world have you yet, my dear, as long as I am alive that is." Concern flowed into his words. "We shall not tarry on this cliff too much longer, lest I not be here the next time, to rescue you from imminent danger."

Her memories of him were all too clear.

The slight breeze smelled of a recent rainfall. The fresh scent of grass and leaves, of water from small streams, all carried to her senses. Wind drifted through the grass, wisping the blades back and forth, along with the neighboring tree branches. Bright green painted every foothill and valley. Wildflowers dotted the terrain with purple, white, and yellow as if spring was an artist who had worked on the land for longer than two weeks.

The "painter" must have been a romanticist—she'd added layers of mist and a thin veil of clouds floating in the sky. The effect allowed Aveline to imagine the height of each summit in turn. Everything around her joined together to provide a hearty welcome, a warm feeling of belonging that she'd missed in her life.

The passengers exited the coach's right side door. The footman took her satchel from the boot and escorted Aveline as far as the graveled walk. Then, after he bade her farewell, she made her way toward the Georgian farmhouse alone, hoping she might belong somewhere at last. The old-fashioned white painted door was unlocked and opened into a small living space where only embers burned in the hearth. She stood in the middle of the floor and peered around the room. She was too tired to care if anyone heard her entrance. The opened windows, with their small green curtains pulled back from the frames, were the only source of lighting. The walls were white-washed and the floor wooden. Chairs and a cushioned settee surrounded the fireplace. Aveline could easily imagine living the rest of her days there.

You can be happy here, just let your mind soar. She could almost hear her father's words in her head as if he was speaking to her from beyond the grave. Yes, she could just imagine him saying something like that.

She left her heavy satchel on the floor and toured the rest of the house. She peered into the small dining room first, with its oval oak table and chairs to match. Next, she looked into the kitchen, with its small stone oven and cooking table. The room smelled like warm apple pie. She was hungry but there were more important matters to look into before she could sit down to a meal in her new home.

Two bedrooms were located on the far left side of the wall, not very well furnished, except for desks, chests of drawers, and beds. She decided those items did not need to be explored in greater detail at the moment.

She found a staircase at the back of the sitting room. Ascending the steep stairs, taking care not to stumble, she found a large master bedroom, decorated with masculine-furnishings. No pastels or floral prints were to be found in any part of it. Instead, deep mahogany, with a touch of green, ornamented the curtains, walls, rug, and quilt.

A sudden wave of sadness hit her as she realized she stood in the same room where her father had stayed. Yes, she looked upon his secret abode at last. Flopping down upon the four-poster bed, she sighed heavily with fatigue from the long journey in the carriage. Although she had slept on the way, it was a choppy sleep at best because of the churning sea and bumpy carriage ride.

She decided to explore the rest of the farm. She rose from the bed and descended the stairs. When she exited the kitchen door, she headed toward the barn. She saw empty fields where she imagined workers plowing with oxen, planting crops, feeding chickens, and putting water in troughs for horses.

She wanted to invite everyone to eat supper together, so she could meet the people who worked for her. She'd never doubt those who her father had hired, but nonetheless, she wanted to know if what Miss McCork said about Irishmen was true.

She peered in the barn door and saw four men with mugs in their hands. They were conversing loudly. In fact, they seemed to be singing, each voice at a different pitch.

"Oh the wearin' o' the green,
"Oh the wearin' o' the green!"

One of the men stood out from the others. His clothing was obviously expensive, despite its poor condition. She stood quietly and observed him through the crack of the door, wondering who he was.

He discarded his brown swallowtail coat and threw it over the stall wall, leaving only a green cotton waistcoat and a worn, white linen shirt covering his upper torso. The shirt hung open, exposing the man's broad chest, dusted with dark hair. The waistcoat, also unbuttoned, trailed down toward brown corduroy trousers that fit snugly around his muscled thighs. His clothes were unmarked by patches, though stains from dirt surrounded both knees. He wore brown stockings with black leather brogues.

Aveline had rarely scrutinized a man so closely in all her life. Why was she doing so

27

to this one? A man she'd not yet become acquainted with. Although, he was facing toward her, she remained unseen.

A little bit more observation of the man wouldn't hurt. After all, I do have a right to know more about who works for me, she mused.

The man's raven hair fell nearly to his shoulders and feathered toward his prominent jaw. His strong chin was set in a manner similar to her father's, indicating a man capable of dealing with all kinds of stress. The arm not holding his mug hung at his side. His posture radiated an air of authority. He was obviously not just any farm laborer. He was inches taller than two of the other three and slim.

His angular nose flared outward and his close-set eyes showed a shimmering light blue. The dimples and high cheekbones were alluring, as were his straight white teeth.

Simply put, the man was breathtaking.

Forcing her gaze away from his countenance, she bowed her head and listened to him lead the singing.

"So if the color we must wear be
England's cruel red,
"Let it remind us of the blood
that Irishmen have shed,
"And pull the shamrock from your hat,
"And trow it on the sod,
"But never fear, it will take root there,
"Though underfoot 'tis trod."

She wanted to stand in the doorway and watch him sing for the rest of the day. His voice was wonderful and its warm tone washed through her. But she knew the longer she remained the more likely it was she'd be seen. As an eavesdropper, she had seen and learned more information than her father would ever have allowed. That is why she loved doing it.

The time grew late and she decided to leave. She'd introduce herself when she wouldn't be an interruption. Her success on the farm revolved around their good opinion of her. Easing away, she stumbled and grabbed a hold of the door, causing it to creak. Suddenly, the Irishman looked directly at her. The grin she'd seen on his face just moments before turned to a scowl.

She did not stick around to see what he did next, but ran in the direction of the farmhouse. He caught her arm in three quick strides, grabbed her wrist, and spoke to her in Gaelic as she turned around, gasping for breath. His language was beautiful. She just wished she understood what he was trying to say.

Chapter 3

C iarán O'Devlin was not fond of trespassers or foreigners, especially the English, and saw defiance in her steady gaze.

But she was pretty. Her copper hair was coiled in a topknot, and a white bonnet adorned with pink flowers covered it. Her small lips puckered fetchingly. Her arched eyebrows, the color of her hair, stood over her golden eyes. The light pink dress framed her small curves. Her bosom was moderately sized as it swelled in the thin muslin gown. Her clothes puzzled him. They were a little too rich for her to be from any of the nearby towns.

What was she doing here of all places?

The English loved to send anyone willing to make a little extra money.

He moved close enough to her to touch her, but she held her ground. "I want to know who you are an' why you are spying on me. If it is such a problem for you to answer then me thinks you should not be here."

She didn't flinch. "My name is Aveline Peyton. I own these lands. I should be asking who you are to question my authority."

Releasing his grip on her arm, he staggered backward a few steps. His eyes narrowed on her, and he breathed more deeply. "A woman who is in charge o' a farm? I have never heard o' such an absurd notion in all me life. I think 'tis past time for you to be going already an'—'em—" Her first words echoed in his head. "Peyton is ya last name, *cailín*?"

She hesitated. "Yes..."

He nodded. "Right, you are related then to the late Lord Peyton?"

Despite her confidence, he noticed a change in her eyes. "I am indeed. His only daughter." When she spoke, she turned her face toward the moors.

He paused to think for a few moments. He had known that if anything happened to Lord Peyton, his daughter would be the heir to all his properties. *Hmm...*

County Tyrone, Ireland, 1821:

When Lord Peyton hailed him to the farmhouse's doorstep, Ciarán had been about to wash his hands outside the barn after a hard day's work. The early evening was still and the sky held the rain that came every night during the spring months. The moisture's pleasant smell filled the air.

Ciarán wanted to be inside before the heavens made their decision.

He frowned. "Leaving so soon?" he asked Lord Peyton. "You have not been here two fortnights."

Lord Peyton cast his countenance downward and gestured for Ciarán to follow him into the front parlor to sit by the hearth. A small fire burned low, making the area around glow red. Miss O'Grace, the maid, entered from the kitchen and handed each man a mug of ale.

"Thank you." Lord Peyton waited for her to skitter away. He smoothed the thighs of his black trousers and lounged into a red velvet-lined mahogany chair seemingly without a care in the world.

Ciarán sat on the settee and sipped his ale.

Lord Peyton drank a hearty sip. "My daughter has written me to return home as soon as possible. A close acquaintance will be holding a luncheon next month. They have an eligible bachelor for a son. No doubt it is the Kinseys." He emphasized the name with a pound of his left fist upon his thigh. "I have a suspicion she will not even consider the gentleman as a suitable husband for her."

"You stated before she refuses anyone who comes to offer for her hand. A smart woman, I say," Ciarán said.

Brown eyes watched him drink. "You state such ideas because you've never considered the idea of marriage."

"Well, 'tis the truth," he agreed.

They laughed.

Lord Peyton's face deepened into a grimace. "To my dismay, I have a position in society to uphold and that cannot be accomplished with an unmarried daughter who is unhappy. Everyone frowns upon the first part, when the second is what bothers me the most. I do not think I should attend this...this..." He faltered in between heavy breaths.

"For Heaven's sakes, man, why do you have to go then?"

"The girl blackmailed me!"

Ciarán sputtered on a sip of ale. "Right, well how was she able to do such a thing?"

The lord pounded another fist onto his thigh. "By writing a letter back to the Kinseys telling them she was attending with no one other than her dear own papa. Certainly not the end of it, mind you."

He became flustered and nearly spilled the ale from his mug. "She went on to tell me if I do not make an appearance, she will not even consider the gentleman at all."

Ciarán suspected the same, but offered another approach. "Methinks you should make an appearance at this luncheon with ya daughter. I know she blackmailed you an' all, but suppose she really likes this son o' theirs?"

Lord Peyton sighed. "I know for a fact she does not."

He sipped a long gulp of the dark liquid. He looked older. His dark brown hair grayed from the sides upward, and the white of his shirt nearly matched his pallor.

Ciarán took a small sip, giving him a smile over the mug. "Well, at least she is giving him a benefit o' the doubt."

"Your words speak truth. She'd never disappoint me in that regard. I am the one who needs convincing though. Atherton Kinsey is a nice young fellow, but he is not the person for someone with so much promise, someone such as my daughter..."

As the lord looked at him, Ciarán nodded in understanding. Lord Peyton's daughter was not the only one rejecting her suitors.

"You are an exceptional young man, O'Devlin," Lord Peyton said. "I know I can trust you to manage this farm for however long I am away."

Pride seeped through Ciarán faster than the alcohol. "'Twill be me honor as always, George. The farm will be waiting for ya return, as well as I."

They finished their ale in silence.

Lord Peyton left the following morning. Ciarán never saw him again.

♕ ♕ ♕

Ciarán wondered why the lord never said his daughter's name. She'd been mentioned in the letter he received from the English solicitor, telling him of Lord Peyton's death and telling him that she was the farm's new owner. The omission seemed pointless now. She was the owner, and he knew rather more about her than he wished.

Turning away, he left her in silence. He made his way to the farmhouse and decided against telling his friends about her arrival. Somehow, Ciarán knew her first meetings with his people would not bode well.

Sitting in his room alone, he felt deeply disappointed. There had to be a mistake. Lord Peyton was his closest friend. To think the farm was not left to him was more painful than a direct slap to his face.

Chapter 4

Aveline sighed and returned to the barn. She would attempt to befriend the other men even if she was unable to befriend the one in charge. She walked through the open door and glanced around. A man piled hay into a horse's stall. The two others were up the ladder, repairing pieces of the loft. No one seemed to have noticed her. They had returned to work upon their leader's hasty departure.

"Hello, my name is Aveline Peyton and I

now own the farm." She spoke in a loud voice, getting their attention immediately. "My father died not a fortnight ago. He believed I would prosper with it. Of course, it is a more complicated matter. I know you are not fond of the English, but I come here upon the wishes of my father. I would much prefer to abide here with friends rather than enemies."

The men seemed flabbergasted. They turned toward her and stared without a word.

She beckoned. "Am I to assume no one is able to speak English here?"

"I do." A tall, burly man came from the corner he'd piled hay into. "*Sassenach*, we dinnae make friends with you. Nor do we abide by ya rules. We are loyal to *an fear* Mr. O'Devlin an' him do we intend ta follow." His words were discernible. He possessed a thicker, more outlandish accent. A Scottish accent.

His reddish hair contrasted with the dark

shade of green in his eyes. A trimmed beard covered his lower jaw. His heavily stained clothing was crusted with dirt from the day's work. His plaid trousers fit a bit too snug.

She blushed. "Would you like to join me for supper tonight, so we may get better acquainted—"

A man interrupted her from the loft. "*Ní me.*"

Another man, his lighter brown hair swishing as he shook his head, possessed the same angry look. Both men had striking blue eyes like their leader.

"Mr. O'Devlin dinnae take kindly ta guests in his farmhouse. If he discovers ye are asking us without his permission, he will surely have all o' our heads," said the red-haired man.

His attempt to dissuade her was not working.

To think one tall, handsome, pushy— Irishman—would make this Scotsman nervous. It was unbelievable!

Aveline placed her hands on her hips. "Since I am now the true owner of the farm, he cannot have a say any longer about the matter."

They looked from one to the other.

"While you are contemplating things, please do tell me your names," she said.

"Nae *Sassenach*, I do not think this is such a grand notion...ta meddle with Mr. O'Devlin's temper is a foul wish."

Surely, this Mr. O'Devlin's temper caused the uneasiness among his people. Was his anger so unforgiving? Why hadn't *she* become frightened yet?

The Scotsman rubbed the hair on his jaw. "The name is Afton MacRory. Up there is Eònan and Sòlas...um...O'Feighry. They are brothers. If 'tis in our best interest ta join you for supper, we will be there. We've more duties ta attend ta before the day ends. Good day ta you, Lady Aveline," Afton said, and turned to continue his work.

She left the barn.

She preferred a different introduction to her workers, but improvements would come with time. Fortunately, Mr. O'Devlin had not approached her when she entered the farmhouse. Her satchel was exactly where she left it and she moved it into an unexplored bedroom.

"What are the likes o' you doing in me master's house?" The diminutive maid spoke with courage. "If you do not explain ya self, I will have to ask you to leave."

Aveline admired her courage. "I do not know why you are asking me this, you should know who I am, but it most certainly does not concern you in the slightest."

The maid scowled. "I may be just a servant, *Sasanach*, but I live here too, an' I won't be having me loyal master's land taken away before me very eyes by someone I don't know." The Irishwoman's eyes had shown more than outrage. She deeply cared about Lord Peyton.

Were Aveline's servants back home as concerned about her? She did not know how to answer such a question. Servants were not friends. They were paid wages to clean the house and serve the food.

What does sasanach have to do with me? "Miss...I do not seem to know your name, but as the farm's landowner, I plan to make my home here."

"Mr. O'Devlin will be none too happy about that fact. His temper can get nasty inna short amount o' time."

She groaned. "So I have heard."

"He already knows about you?" The maid sounded wistful.

Aveline smiled. She knew a way to gain the maid's trust. "Of course he does. Why, we met earlier today in the barn. I am surprised you were not informed of my arrival."

The Irishwoman shook her cap-covered

hair. "Come on, he'd be upset if 'twas the case."

"Oh, he is very upset," Aveline pointed out. "But as you can see, I have all the hairs still on my head."

The maid held in her laughter. Her warm smile surprised Aveline. "I s'pose ya right 'bout that. Me name's Sinéad O'Grace. I am loyal to the late master and his manager, but I hope you do not hold it against me."

She nodded. "I am Lady Aveline Peyton. It is a pleasure to make your acquaintance, Miss O'Grace." The maid went to turn around, but halted her steps when Aveline spoke. "Oh, please do tell me when supper is and what we are to eat. I am very famished."

Sinéad chuckled. "I am makin' boxty an' some barmbrack. The Kerry apple cake in the oven is for dessert. The cake is O'Devlin's favorite, you know. Potatoes an' bread are not something you eat much over-seas, is it?"

Aveline frowned toward the front door. "He will not be joining us."

"Who are you talkin' 'bout, lady?" Miss O'Grace asked.

"Why, O'Devlin, of course."

"He's very upset after all, I s'pose." It was a statement, not a question.

"Yes, I believe so." She lowered her head. "So I have invited the other men to join us."

Miss O'Grace headed toward the kitchen. "In that case, I will need ta triple me recipe."

Before supper, Aveline went into her room, sat at her desk, and started writing her new novel. She'd unpack in the morning.

A man stood in the doorway and Blythe Compton scrutinized his appearance. He wore a very elegant black evening suit. His frock hung upon a peg near the door and he leaned toward the side with an exuded look of confidence. The man's raven hair reached his neck in a short style, his locks hung just over his eyes. The sky reflected in them a pale shade of blue, as he smiled upon her with a dimpled grin. He was a handsome man indeed. No aristocrat she'd ever known greeted visitors at the door...but he was a very different kind of man.

Aveline smiled. The words were a wonderful start.

👑 👑 👑

Ciarán took his meal upstairs. He would not allow the Englishwoman to see his feelings in such turmoil. She came from such a different culture than his—a city brimming with men and women in fashionable garb and high paid servants catering to every whim. He knew none of those luxuries, and had grown up learning all about life through experience.

The aristocracy troubled in understanding about hard work and the fruits of labor. Instead they pursued artistic endeavors, and watched everyone else toil on their behalf. Throughout history, the Irish were forced to relinquish their culture and language. Land tied his people to the country, sowed seeds to support the nation, and kept hopes alive for a future without partition. Ciarán woke up each day to work and secure the land for future generations.

Lady Aveline had looked lost, even forlorn, when he'd met her. He finished eating. The sad emotions reminded him to forget about the woman. He wished Lord Peyton had never died. He would still have a friend, but *he* would manage the farm. He could at least prevent Lady Aveline from roaming in his thoughts if nothing else.

He wiped his mouth on a cloth and quietly went down stairs to eavesdrop on her.

Hypocrisy was his favorite therapy.

Chapter 5

Later in the evening, Aveline sat alone at the supper table. She heard not a single human voice. The maid clattered pots and pans in the kitchen, and she wondered if anyone would come to dinner at all. Mr. O'Devlin would not be there. She glanced around the small room and worried whether her invitation was as friendly as she'd intended.

She remembered a similar predicament a time long before.

County Cumbria, England, 1821:

Aveline had talked vigorously to her mother's portrait above the fireplace. "He told me he would be home by morning." She paced the large drawing room. "It's nearly midday and I'm finding it impossible to believe we could arrive at the luncheon on time. Did he perchance send a letter with a change of mind? My father would not tell me what I wish to hear, when his heart deems him to do otherwise."

The sitting room had been her mother's favorite place to read. Her tastes resided in the room's decor long after she passed on. Her father's last visit in the room had left the stench of cigar smoke. A splash of green leaves was imprinted upon the white papered walls. Two light green settees sat in the middle with a miniature table in between. They were all made from the same painted white oak. The single candelabrum on the table provided enough light to sustain suitable illumination. The chairs in the room—one stood near the window and another near a small bookcase—matched the settee. The books on the shelves were coated in dust. No one touched them until her father returned.

"If only you were here, Mama, I would not be alone any longer." About to cry, she heard a door open and close. She turned to see who arrived. "Papa, you are home at last!" Aveline felt the sudden urge to run and wrap her arms around him, exactly the same way she had always greeted him as a little girl. Instead she walked closer, and simply planted a chaste kiss upon his stubbly cheekbone.

He frowned, but immediately recovered. "So I am. I see you spending time with your mother. Is she doing well?"

She gripped her father's proffered arm

and walked with him into the hallway. "Yes, she is well indeed. Did your trip fare well?"

Her father rubbed his sideburns. A sign that he was thinking heavily. "Gravelly, but grand all the same," he said, using terms she'd never heard before. "I believe we shall be on our way to the Kinseys. I am sure Atherton will be delighted to see you once more."

He escorted her to the door and helped her into her patterned shawl. The garment was made with lilac-colored designs, which were the perfect tones to match her dark purple skirts. "Being fashionably late is better than not being there at all."

After a short ride in the carriage, they arrived at the Kinsey Estate and were led directly to the dining hall. Atherton sat near his parents. He glanced at Aveline as she entered. Her father went to stand with the other men. A flush filled her cheeks when every eye in the room followed her arrival.

County Tyrone, Ireland, 1823:

Aveline contemplated skipping supper. As she waited another five minutes, a clatter of loud noise came from the doorway. She stood to peer around the dining room's corner and her heart hammered in her chest. They'd come after all. Anticipation ran through her veins as Mr. MacRory and the brothers walked through the door. They conversed in a loud manner.

The men nodded in her direction and sat themselves around the table. The head chair remained bare.

She could not eat her meal in silence. "Good evening, men. Thank you for joining me."

The brothers grunted in answer.

Then Afton's bold question caught her off guard. "Lady Aveline, are the farm and lands everything you expected them to be?

She liked the farm, but her feelings toward the country were hard to convey.

Miss O'Grace gave her a wide grin.

A potato fell off the fork she held in midair. She knew that her time to respond was drawing to an end, and the farmers desired her answer sooner than later. "Yes, I find this farm and lands very agreeable to my tastes."

The whole room erupted with raucous laughter.

Mr. MacRory stopped laughing and spoke in a serious tone. "This farm, Lady Aveline, will be more than just agreeable to ya tastes. It's ya new way o' life."

♔ ♔ ♔

Ciarán watched the meal silently from the doorway. The Englishwoman's response to such a hard question proved she was a novice to the lands he'd spent his whole life working. He sworn to stand by his words, but seeing her and hearing her speak made him regret the decision.

He remembered a time over five years ago when he thought for himself. He would escape his past when he traveled to the pub and spent time with the barmaid. But after Molly learned his name, she knew too much information about him, and she left.

His work then became his main source of escape from reality. The farm became the one constant in his life he knew how to control, and the only pastime that would keep his mind off of everything he had become responsible to manage. Then, Lady Aveline arrived, and his thoughts about his life changed.

Before she spoke again, he removed himself to his bedchamber, knowing he'd spend another night alone.

The next day, Aveline woke early and missed Mr. O'Devlin at breakfast. The local rector knocked upon the door and requested a meeting to sign the farm's ownership papers. He did not ask questions nor did he remain in the house for long.

Afterwards, she returned to her bedchamber to unpack her satchel and work on her novel. Sitting at the desk, her mind filled with more story ideas than she could write. Unfortunately, every thought revolved around the Irishman. Since her fateful meeting with him the previous day, he truly avoided her.

No doubt he loathed her for being English. The way he shunned her indicated a deeper motive. Maybe she reminded him too much of her father. They had to have been close. She was determined to discover the truth one day.

Mr. O'Devlin was more stubborn than she. He wouldn't allow her to live happily on the farm in his presence. Nonetheless, she found him to be a handsome man and his smile charmed her. Well, his looks charmed her tastes a bit too much. She wished her father's prodigy more resembled Afton who was witty and sociable. She and Afton had talked at length during supper. Maybe he'd be able to help her learn about farming.

She sat at the worn desk and grasped an ink quill. An idea hurtled through her mind from thin air, and she looked for an empty spot on the paper to write. Pieces of paper were scattered over the desk. She grabbed one and started to write. Details rose to the surface and formed into sentences. She filled in the blank page with another person's life. A life she felt she'd lived before.

Blythe stared at him.
He ended the silence between them with an inquiry. "May I ask why you pay me an unsolicited visit to Stanford

Hall? Surely you have not received an invitation."

"No, sir, I do not have an invitation. I saw an ad in the local newspaper and it stated you may have a vacancy for a housemaid," she said.

"A housemaid you say? I have not needed one of those since..." He stopped his words abruptly, continuing in a more subdued manner. "Yes, well, it seems you have arrived at the most opportune time. Come along now, before the chill weather leaves you ill."

He did not wish for the confused expression on her face to spur an onslaught of questions. If she pushed her limits, he might change his mind.

"Thank you very much, sir." The simple answer was enough to calm his ill thoughts.

"Since you are a new member of

my employ, it would be splendid if I knew what name to call you." He watched as she removed her bonnet and cloak, placing them next to his frock on the peg. Her golden hair was pulled back into a severe bun at the crown and two curling tendrils framed her face. The woman's eyes shone sea green as she assessed the manse she would make her new home.

She turned her eyes from the large entrance hall back to him. "They call me Blythe, well Blythe Compton rather. What shall I call you?"

He remained in the doorway, smirking. "I am Lord Vincent Stanford, Earl of Lancaster. I will have my man show you to your chambers, and then you may meet with the housekeeper. She will show you the chores."

He wondered how such a hand-

some woman read the newspaper article he had written over a year ago. He could not believe anyone with such proper manners and a rich countenance as she possessed, would find herself into servitude for a lonely lord. Some questions were better left unanswered or even asked, he shrugged. His butler closed the door behind them.

Lord Vincent walked up the large staircase leading into his study, turning in mid-step. "Good day to you, Miss Compton." He bowed to her and left before she could reply.

A few moments later, the footman greeted Blythe from the entranceway. "Good day, Miss Compton. Shall I show you to your chambers?"

She followed him behind the staircase into the servants' quarters. "That would be splendid. Thank you." Lord

Vincent's presence lingered in her mind. The loneliness about him spurred her to believe he'd lived a hard life, despite the riches he presently surrounded himself with.

"My name is Mr. Edmund Thornton." His voice echoed down the long hallway.

The manse felt eerie, but she determined to make the best of a better situation.

Aveline immersed herself completely into writing. She nearly forgot lunch. But when the time arrived, she hoped Mr. O'Devlin would be there.

👑 👑 👑

Afton MacRory sauntered over to where his friend tilled the field for wheat and oats. "I need some land for the lass, O'Devlin."

Sweat dripped down the Irishman's brow in beads and collected dirt along the way. "The colleen will not be doing any work for me farm."

"The lass wants ta work. She told me herself she did. It would seem she could give us a wee hand, so that we dinnae have such a heavy load. Do ya ken?"

"O'course, MacRory, I understand our load would be lessened. She knows nothing about farming, though." O'Devlin leaned against the plow handles, he'd worked straight past breakfast, and the lack of sleep from the previous night showed through the purple circles under his eyes. "Women are hard ones to teach."

His forearms tipped the oxen cart too hard, causing the animal to jolt with the sudden movement. He almost toppled over onto the ground, catching himself at the last minute.

Afton started to laugh. *Mr. O'Devlin*

needs to relax a bit. Maybe this woman is here for a reason.

O'Devlin scowled. "Get anything you blather about later out o' ya head!"

"'Tis gone with the wind, O'Devlin." His chest heaved as he held in more laughter, wondering how the man knew what he'd been thinking.

"I am glad to hear it."

Afton rubbed his bristly jaw. "You know, O'Devlin, I can teach her if you dinnae mind givin' me a piece o' land ta work with."

"Done."

O'Devlin continued working.

Afton wished his friend would cease. "What is that s'pose ta mean? You told me I could not have the land before. What changed ya mind?"

"You may have the land, but you must keep the colleen out o' me sight. You can have the few acres over across the way." O'Devlin pointed toward the complete opposite of where he stood. "Near the farm-house."

"Is that what you really want, lad?"

"Yes, I believe it is." No emotion escaped the Irishman's countenance.

Afton would not give up. "Would you like ta join everyone for the noontime meal then?"

"No, there is much to do. I will have me own share when everyone else clears the table." O'Devlin looked toward the ground. "As for now, I shall sow all the oat seeds before the day is out."

Afton nodded a farewell and headed toward the farmhouse. O'Devlin had diverted the conversation as soon as he mentioned Lady Aveline. Why? For an Englishwoman, her beauty and wit enthralled him. Did these qualities have the same effect on the Irishman?

If so, O'Devlin hid those feelings well. *Too* well for Afton's tastes.

Chapter 6

On her third day in Ireland, Aveline awoke at dawn and dressed herself in a faded day gown she found in her dresser. She ate a hearty Irish breakfast with pancakes, eggs, two types of sausages, toast, and apple jelly. No one objected to her early morning presence at the dining table. She put on an old bonnet and walked out the door, following the men toward the barn.

A heavy mist surrounded the hills. The morning was chill, but she knew the temperature would rise as time progressed into the afternoon. No need for a cloak.

She watched Afton gather a feed bag for the horses that were let out of their stalls. The day before, she asked him to teach her how to farm. He knew English well enough and she hoped he'd stay true to his word.

On the other hand, Mr. O'Devlin continued to avoid her at every opportunity. He had eaten in his room for two days. She only saw him from a distance, because he worked in the fields farthest from the house, but the Irishman with the sky blue eyes never left her mind.

She'd waited long enough to take on her duties. Step one was to learn how to farm.

"Pardon my intrusion, Mr. MacRory," she said and paused as she gathered enough courage to continue. "Is there anything I can do to lend a hand with the chores? I refuse to sit everyday while I have workers straining in the heat."

He turned. "Work on a farm is very hard, Lady Aveline. Those soft wee hands o' yas will become rough with calluses. You can always change ya mind. Do ya ken?"

She admired his honesty, above all else.

She drew her hands up and stared at them as she talked. "You will learn all too well, Mr. MacRory, once I get myself into something, it is very hard to persuade me to do otherwise. My hands have grown bored and tired over the years. The last few days are no exception. I do not think it will matter in the least there are calluses on them for once."

He looked at her with a wry smile. "Very well. I know o' something you can do. Let us be gettin' started then."

Afton went through all the steps with Aveline. He told her the names of the farm equipment, —the hoe, the pitchfork, the wheelbarrow, and the sickle. He showed her where they each kept in the barn and their uses.

"Remember, lass, every bit o' work we do on the farm helps for the greater cause. 'Tis why I have this patch o' land for you. Mr. O'Devlin told me I could use this section for whatever I deemed necessary. I have chosen it specifically for crops. Since you are now me new landlady an' all, I s'pose all the land 'tis yas to do what ya like with." The last part he said in a hushed manner.

Aveline nodded in agreement. She wanted to ask so many questions, but didn't know where to start.

Afton explained the first step in farming crops, called tillage. He showed her how to maneuver the ox, guiding the animal harnessed to a plough along the ground to loosen and aerate the first row of soil. Then he watched and laughed as the ox pulled her along by the single plough handle.

The ox jerked wildly out of her control. "Oh no! Mr. MacRory, I do not believe this is what the animal is supposed to do! Can I please get some assistance?"

Eventually, with the Scotsman's aid, the plow broke the top soil and created furrows. She felt her skin burn, despite the cloud cover. Her bonnet had long fallen off her head during the struggle with the ox.

Already, work took a lot of physical strength from her, but she determined to persevere. After an hour's worth of resistance, she maintained the ox at a steady pace.

He grabbed another ox and hitched it to a plough then tilled the stretch of land on the opposite side of the field. Before she could reach the halfway point, he was finished with his side and a good half of hers. The acre of ground was ready for sowing.

"You still have not told me what we will be growing here," Aveline said with labored breathing, pointing a hand toward the tilled field. Hunger pains swept through her stomach.

"Barley. The O'...O'Feighry's are in

charge o' takin' care o' the animals. O'Devlin is watchin' o'er the wheat an' oats he planted two days ago. The time for barley crop is here now." Afton pushed a wheelbarrow carrying a large sack of seeds from the barn.

"We will continue where we left off after luncheon." He set the bag onto the ground. With a relieved smile, she walked to the wash barrel and cleaned her dirty hands.

At the table, she received very unnerving looks from the brothers. Their expressions showed they wished she was not around. *Maybe they did not like women who worked.*

They all ate a hearty pot of rice and barley soup and walked back into the fields.

Afton showed her how the barley seeds were placed into the soil by hand.

She tried to lift the heavy sack on her own but found the feat impossible. So she transported the seeds around the field using the wheelbarrow.

In the last few hours before sunset, she and Afton used the backs of shovels to cover the seeds with the turned up soil. Afton told her this prevented the birds from eating the seeds before they sprouted.

By the time suppertime came, she was sunburned and exhausted. Her pale skin had fared poorly. The sky had remained unclouded throughout the afternoon, leaving a reddish glow upon her neck and shoulders.

Aveline retired to her chambers after another supper without Mr. O'Devlin's presence. She set down a cup of black tea. Upon Miss O'Grace's suggestion, she dipped a clean linen cloth into the brew and applied the cooled liquid onto her burnt skin. Before falling asleep, she wrote a few paragraphs of her budding novel.

Blythe rarely saw the master. Lord Stanford traveled for many days at a time tending to his estate business. The housekeeper, Mrs. Whitlock, showed her how to turn beds and dust the furniture. Her current work saved her thoughts from wandering to her previous life...

After losing their father to illness, Blythe and her brother, Leighton, lived together in their estate. Leigh found a wife and he did not want his unmarried younger sister to live under his roof. Unfortunately, she was his ward and remained with him until either she came of age or married. She had not a single place or person to turn to.

Her brother was the devil. He had locked her in the attic and a servant had come to her once a day to drop off a few victuals and drink. She slept up-

on a small cot, and the tick mattress swallowed her into the center after lying upon it a while.

Blythe abided those lowly conditions for two years before she found any hope her life would change.

She had held the news post containing her father's obituary. Every day she read its contents. The sorrowful account of his life brought tears to her eyes.

She threw the newspaper onto the floor and sat to scratch poetry into the wooden wall with a rock. Her favorite pastime had become writing verse.

> *If there ever was a rose,*
> *Not a portrait of beauty,*
> *It shall never be found,*
> *For all the days I lived,*
> *None such flower exists.*
> *Not anywhere in Heaven,*

May such a bloom be,
For only on Earth is there a sad
rose.

Blythe threw the rock aside. She was in a bout of sadness. The words affected her. Thinking twice, she bent to pick up the rock, and saw the news-paper's ad. The headline read "Earl of Lancaster In Need of Aid." She read the contents and knew she had found a way to escape.

Chapter 7

Aveline took care of the seeds daily. The barley sprouts had pushed through by the end of the week and two-inch shoots with three leaves grew after a fortnight. After the ground was harrowed and rolled, she learned how to use clay pipes to drain the field after irrigation. The draining process took most of an afternoon. She prepared fertilizer from cow manure without flinching and walked through the rows making sure each sprout thrived without fear of weed or pest.

She sang a beautiful Irish tune as she wheeled the barrow full of manure up and down the rows. Her governess, Miss McCork, had taught her the lyrics to a peaceful melody she recognized from childhood.

"'Tis the last rose of summer
"Left blooming alone.
"All her lovely companions
"Are faded and gone.
"No flower of her kindred,
"No rosebud is nigh,
"To reflect back her blushes,
"To give sigh for sigh."

Ciarán stood behind a barn wall listening to every word of her lovely song. He remembered the ballad from his childhood.

She sang beautifully. Every note captivated his senses, taking control of his body like a potion. A woman's voice had never touched his soul so deeply before.

He watched as the days progressed and she took diligent care of the barley. He worked in the fields on the far side of the farm and wondered if she thought about him.

Aveline was never deterred from her duties. During the day, dirt caked upon her clothing, her exposed skin reddened from the clouded sun, but she finished every chore before sundown. She affected him.

She sang as she tended the barley and he savored the sweet sound of her voice.

"I'll not leave thee, thou lone one,
"To pine on the stem.
"Since the lovely are sleeping,
"Go, sleep thou with them.
"Thus kindly I scatter,
"Thy leaves o'er the bed,

Where thy mates of the garden
"Lie scentless and dead."

Ciarán recalled the past two weeks. He was jealous that Afton spent more time with her but he admitted it was for the better.

She sang each word with so much emotion and longing. He could fill the gap for her, but he knew his rightful place. They were hardly acquainted and intimacy would hinder their lives.

Nonetheless, a voice in his mind told him to learn more about her.

She wouldn't possibly speak to him after he vowed to avoid her. Now he needed her presence more than anything. Maybe she'd forgive him for what he said.

Walking closer to Aveline, trying not to frighten her with his proximity, he sang the last verse in a tenor duet with her soprano.

"So soon may I follow,

"When friendships decay,
"From Love's shining circle
"The gems drop away.
"When true hearts lie withered
"And fond ones are flown,
"Oh! Who would inhabit,
"This bleak world alone?
"This bleak world alone..."

Aveline turned as the last line echoed back in a man's voice. Her heart fluttered. "I thought you made it very clear we should not see or talk to each other—" She halted as the air around her became thicker. She felt a silent connection to the Irishman.

Twilight settled in around them.

"So I did." He chuckled, looking toward the ground. "Something about you strikes odd to me though, *cailín*."

She wondered why he thought she was

odd. "Whatever could that be, Mr. O'Devlin, for surely I have not done anything to upset you."

She knew she was more headstrong than most women, but obstinacy does not make a person odd. If anything, he could be labeled as odd, too. A stubborn man who devotes his life to a farm? Bah!

A frown creased his brow. "Nay."

His eyes met hers and she felt the glow of blue fire on her face. "In truth, you have done far more than I ever expected from you."

Well, overcoming an Irishman's expectations is very difficult indeed. "Did you really think, Mr. O'Devlin, I would run and hide from you? I am not a coward, if that is what you are saying."

His eyes widened. "Right, you are not a coward." His soft words washed through her. "Ya singing voice is quite brilliant."

"I'm glad the fact is now established."

Maybe he gave a compliment to weaken her. "It is only a voice after all. Certainly not something to get eager about—"

He pushed her doubts into the dirt. "Nonsense! You highly underestimate..."

Every word he spoke made her weak at the knees, so she ignored him and turned toward the wheelbarrow instead.

"I should finish my duties before it is time to wash for supper. The days go by so fast as of late. It was only this morning when I was helping the brothers feed the animals—" She bent to place the last item in the wheelbarrow, lost her balance and fell against the handles. The cart tipped, losing its contents. She fell backward into his embrace.

Setting her upright, Mr. O' Devlin pulled her around, gently moved the hair off her face, and kissed her full on the mouth.

Aveline tasted like honey and melted like butter in Ciarán's arms.

He could not stand there and let her prattle on about chores, when all he had wanted to do since the day they met was press his lips against hers. She captivated him, and he felt drawn to her. They were trapped in a sea of emotions. The very passion he refused to experience with an Englishwoman. If he opened his heart, she would rush in, and the order he fought so hard to maintain would be lost. She would become his constant focus, and his people would suffer for his actions.

After all, 'tis only a kiss and nothing more, he thought.

He'd survived this long without more from a woman. A single kiss would not count for anything.

Then darkness enveloped them while supper grew cold on the table.

Chapter 8

I would very much like to know how you and my father became acquainted, Mr. O'Devlin," Aveline said as she walked with him to the fields lying along the River Blackwater.

After the previous day's events, it was no wonder they were trying to form a friendship. And surely he welcomed a picnic after making hay bundles of the autumn wheat crop.

He placed a crimson tartan on the ground.

When the farmers broke for luncheon, she had traded her soiled work clothes for a collared chemise with double ruffles and an overskirt made of sheer muslin. The whole ensemble was forest green, but she wrapped a black shawl over her shoulders. She hadn't the money for full mourning attire like propriety demanded. Afterwards, she placed a wide-brimmed bonnet with green ribbons on her head. The hat left a mass of fiery ringlets framing her face, with the rest of her hair in a looped bun pinned in the back.

She felt too overdressed for a picnic outdoors, but her outfit was the closest to a riding dress she had with her and she wanted to look presentable.

At least he had smiled when she met him at the barn.

Sitting on the blanket, she felt a sudden heat wash through her. She couldn't forget the way her body had warmed to his kiss. A blush rose to her cheeks. A soft breeze wafted from the moors. Her dress flapped with abandon in the slight wind.

"'Tisn't something you would enjoy knowing about me life." He stared down at the potato farl in his hands.

Miss O'Grace had packed many in their basket. A large jug of ale sat between them.

"I am sure there is much I do not know, but please enlighten me on this aspect of your life. I miss my father so dearly." She looked into the distance, hoping a small ray of sunshine amongst a sea of clouds would glitter upon the water. The sparkle of light would illuminate the dark surface, lightening the bleakness of their conversation.

She saw the wind sweep through his raven hair and noted his sullen expression. She measured his pause. Would he tell her what she most wanted to hear?

"When I was but a lad—" he started.

Her laughter rang out. "Oh, Mr. O'Devlin, you are still a young man!"

"Right, on the day we do not wear a clover on St. Patty's, I will believe I am still young. Surely, Lady Aveline, I feel nearly two score!"

She shook her head. "You do not look it. One score and eight certainly do not equal two score in your case, Mr. O'Devlin."

"Well, youth is a blessed feeling I mean number, then."

Her laughter continued.

"When I was a younger lad, more than I am today..." He winked, giving her a grin full of dimples.

Her laughter subsided, and she fanned her face to keep from swooning.

His smile fell. "Me parents an' me two sisters died o' the consumption."

Consumption? How dreadful! Sadness enveloped her. Sadness for him. He had lost four family members to the horrible infection. Her mother had died in childbirth and her father of liver disease. She knew the pain of loss and all she could do was encourage him to continue talking. She smiled, though her eyes filled with tears.

He gulped the ale, and she knew unshed grief swamped him. "I worked the land with me two brothers for long hours every day until they passed. The three o' us lived with me Gran until the Earth took her a few years later. I never knew how I managed not to contract the disease from me parents, but I was thankful for being able to live."

He paused, and it allowed Aveline to reflect on his words. He was right. The disease was highly contagious. Well, she was also glad to be alive.

He spoke in a more subdued manner. "After Gran, I survived on the streets, fending for meself alone. Me brothers went to a workhouse to make a living. I preferred to stay behind and fight for me family's land."

She took advantage of another pause. "I daresay you made the right decision."

His face became a shadowy mask. "Indeed. My ancestors had worked on it for many decades. One poor year for crops, an' me employer was forced to sell the land to an Englishman who paid a very high price for the lot. I was about five years o' age then. He sent me to grammar school, an' when I was old enough he sent me along to Trinity, where they taught me English. All the while he treated me like his own son."

Noticing the change in his facade, she knew of whom he spoke. "My papa!"

"Right, you are."

Her father's cheerful countenance came to mind. Every smile he gave brightened his whole face, crinkling the corners of his eyes. Wrinkles in those corners were commonly caused by age, but in Lord Peyton's case, mirth was the creator. She wondered if Mr. O'Devlin glimpsed the same reflection in her smile. Why did he sit so close?

Then she regained her senses. "He'd

leave for such a long time, and I would worry immensely about him, but I am glad he remained happy while he stayed here."

His head shook. "Ya father never remained here long though, I'm afraid. After less than a few months' time, he asked me to run the farm in his stead, explaining he wanted to return to you."

She giggled.

He pointed playfully into her direction. "Ya father always mentioned you when we talked. The man was Atlas, an' you were his whole world."

He watched her.

Aveline bowed her head and reflected on his words. "Where are your brothers? For surely they know you have the old family farm back."

His eyes never left hers. "I believe there is a story for that one, too. You see, me eldest brother looked for me shortly after I graduated from Trinity. He spent three years in the workhouse with our other brother, an' none o' them felt happiness there. So the time came for them to reunite with family an' try for a better life. Me brother simply went into a local pub an' asked if anyone had seen the likes o' me. He was immediately directed to Altmore Farm."

"Have I met them yet? Your brothers?" she asked.

"Yes, you have met Eònan and Sòlas. They work on the farm."

Her mouth gaped open. "They did not share your last name. Without familiarity, it is impossible to guess one's identity, nonetheless family relations." She remembered the two men Mr. MacRory introduced to her and she chastised herself for not guessing the truth sooner.

"'Tis rather odd you would mention such a notion. They were o' me same blood, o' course they shared me last name. Unless..." He looked behind him toward the barn.

"MacRory was on the defensive about me name. You see, he's a friend o' me brothers from the workhouse, with Scottish blood through an' through. He did not trust the English an' knew his loyalties were to lie under my leadership." He took a swig of ale and finished his last potato cake.

She ate a farl, and washed it down with wine from a separate jug. "I have a problem, Mr. O'Devlin, with figuring out why you distrust the English so much. Everybody who works on this farm calls me by the name of *sass-ah-naach,* and somehow I feel as if they are disdainful toward me."

He swallowed the last bite of potato. "*Sass-en-knack* is our language for English-man or in your case, Englishwoman. My people call you what you really are, *cailín.*" He corrected her pronunciation of the word in Gaelic. "In me own opinion, I love just calling you a girl.

"The English, ya people, are coming over

an' taking many of me people's farmland to pay for high taxes. He was a great man, but ya father was no exception. I became lucky enough to be under his protection."

Aveline's face glowed with her appreciation.

"Be it as it may," he said and sighed. "There were other such incidents where me people were forcefully taken from their land, losing their lives in the process. We can forgive the English for that, *och* to forget, is impossible."

She wished her heart didn't thump every time he flashed his charming grin. The rapid beating in her chest triggered more than just apprehension. She became more aware of his overwhelming presence as his gaze bore a secret passage deep into her soul. She needed to escape before he dived in.

She rose from the blanket, leaving him sprawled on the plaid. The Irish breeze sent her hat flying and she welcomed the diversion. She ran across the grass in an attempt to catch her bonnet, as it skidded toward the water's edge, leaving O'Devlin behind on the blanket.

Chapter 9

Ciarán couldn't help but laugh at her feeble attempts to capture the bonnet. The smile upon her face reminded him of the times he poured cold water onto his brothers' sleeping heads. Although they were incensed, Éonan and Solás laughed with him at breakfast. He missed childhood.

Aveline looked at home on the moors. Her carefree expression indicated she belonged on the lands.

He could not keep his eyes off the woman. His heartbeat picked up in anticipation when she almost caught the bonnet. Then, a mist clouded over his vision. The obstruction cleared with an image of a similar woman, except this time, she chased after a child instead of a scruff of material.

Surely, his eyes deceived him. The young girl was beautiful. She wore a flowing white muslin gown, and her long black hair cascaded down her back. She ran around on the grass with a rose cradled close to her heart. The short stem was held in between her tiny hands. She looked behind her. Her eyes shone with a mischievous twinkle and were the same shade as his. He didn't know what he'd do if the child looked at him.

The titian-haired woman called to the girl. "You get back here!"

Ciarán felt as if he'd drunk too much ale. The vision was outlandish. He didn't have a daughter, nor did Aveline. He'd certainly remember if anything compromising had occurred between them.

The little girl unsettled him. He sensed an uncanny connection to her. An inside feeling convinced him to accept the child as his daughter and Lady Aveline as her mother. The girl looked fatigued, as she leaned against a nearby rock. Her chest heaved with exhaustion. He watched as the woman picked the little girl up in her arms.

"I have got you at last!" She heavily breathed, cradling the child to her breast. She walked over to him with the small bundle, holding her burden out to him. "Ciarán..."

The girl was fast asleep in her arms.

Did he hear her call him by name?

"Mr. O'Devlin?" Her words cut into his dream world.

His vision misted over once more and the little girl was replaced by the clear sight of the rumpled bonnet in her arms. "What is this, *cailín*?"

He felt groggy, like he just awoke from sleep.

Aveline gestured, while handing the bonnet over to him. "Could you place this over there for me so it does not blow away again? I nearly lost my favorite bonnet to the beautiful river water. I would not want to chance it being lost to me forever."

He grabbed the round piece of cloth from her hands and placed it securely under the basket. "There you go."

"Thank you," she said, before silence enveloped them.

Ciarán couldn't help but reflect on the heart-wrenching daydream he witnessed, an experience which seemed all too real. He never considered marriage in his lifetime. Well, ever since he found his purpose, the farm.

He refused to succumb to women's wiles. Ever since Molly tossed him from her life years ago, he had relinquished the notion of intimacy with a woman altogether. He had risked his heart once, and he did not plan on repeating the pain again. Although, he saw a brighter tomorrow in the Englishwoman's eyes, marriage was an improbable risk due to his status in Irish society.

His whole life was dedicated to the farm and providing his people with food and security. According to them, he worked far too much and would not bestow enough time to a family. A union with her would show a weakness he did not wish for others to see. A man cannot live his life for others without someone around who will only live for him. Was she thinking of him?

Ciarán again saw her image with his child in her arms and knew Aveline hadn't shared the same vision. Why would he daydream such a vivid one-sided illusion? Did he glimpse his future? What was the little girl's significance? The questions came too quickly for him to answer.

He ignored the fact as long as he could bear, until he concluded his feelings were definitely possessive for the woman beside him, clothed in the color of his people. Green brought out the red in her hair, and the amber in her eyes. She didn't wear mourning like other women who lost a close relative, but black wouldn't suit her as well.

He shook his head and lifted the jug into the air. "This is some good ale." He knew he drank too much and blamed his current state for the vision, but the admission did not answer the questions plaguing him. Lowering his arm, he looked over at Aveline.

She laughed. "Then we shall be glad there is no more. I want to hear a story, Mr. O'Devlin."

He was relieved she did not wish to know his thoughts. Her hair was loose, a streak of dirt was on her forehead, and a small grass stain marked the side of her dress. Her dishevelment appealed to him and he needed to find another way to occupy his eyes. "I already told you one, *cailín*." He looked toward the river, wondering if a cold dip would clear his senses from the insanity of marriage clouding not only his mind, but—

To his surprise, she did not hesitate. "No, I want to hear one about your people."

His eyes roamed to her. She planted herself upon the blanket next to him and leaned back, stretching her legs out. Her mouth curved toward the right side of her cheek in a mischievous smile. The loose copper curls on her neck shined, as they swayed like chimes in the wind.

He smelled her scent in the air, lavender. The tantalizing aroma relaxed him and he sank into the familiar emotional quicksand. He should not be so smitten after a single day spent on a picnic together. He needed to say something—anything—before his brain registered the unspoken question.

"It is time to get back to the farm."

Ciarán looked at the sky, noticing the time at half-past one in the afternoon. A rain cloud dipped toward them. It would rain this night. "There is much work to do before the day is out."

Her voice took on a very serious tone as he stood from the blanket. "No. First, I shall hear your story and then we can return to the farm before the rains come. Our time together is most certainly not over yet, Mr. O'Devlin."

The change in her voice caught his attention. Her smile vanished like the sun behind a cloud. She wasn't in the mood to argue with him.

"I catch ya drift, Lady Aveline. We will stay longer if it so pleases you." He loved her straight-forward attitude and wanted to spend time in her presence. What could another half-hour hurt? "Let me see. Have you heard the tale about the Morríghan?"

"My governess spoke of her briefly when I was a child. Who is she?"

A sense of pride washed over him, knowing he'd captured her attention. "There once lived a beautiful woman who walked the moors near Lough Neagh, along the mountains o' Pomeroy where no one saw her. The only scrap o' clothing she wore consisted of a long black cloak with a hood to cover her head."

Aveline apparently liked to ask questions. "If no one saw her, how did they know she was beautiful?"

He smiled, rose and walked a few feet away. "Her beauty was proclaimed by the way she presented herself. The townspeople only saw her in the late evenings, though at a far distance, an' so they gave her a name. The people called her Morríghan, meaning "phantom queen." I've heard talk of her having long raven hair an' eyes o' the lightest o' blues. The color of which is mistaken for gray. Although a goddess, Morríghan wasn't free from human emotions."

No one is. "She fell in love with a soldier named Cúchulainn who fought in the fields near where she roamed. In order for her to tell him how she felt, she revealed herself to people who did not believe she existed."

Ciarán did not return to the blanket, nor did he move from his stance on the grass.

♛ ♛ ♛

Aveline watched him intently. His clothing looked clean. Maybe he dressed for the occasion, too. "Being in a large society, I know how challenging it is opening one's self to so much ridicule. Especially to those who judge upon looks alone."

He grimaced at the lack of ale in the jug. The man never complained about anything aloud. He was a leader who got his point across through actions. His manner exuded more respect and responsibility than his words ever could.

"'Twas very hard for her. So, she took the form o' a crow, flying above the battlefield to watch her beloved. She appeared to him four times in an attempt for him to notice her, but Cú did not. He dedicated every emotion an' every aspect o' himself to the training instead."

Aveline watched him set the jug into the basket, and walked ten paces to the river to drink some water. "One day when he was alone in the woods, eating supper, she appeared to him an' let down the hood of her cloak. Morríghan told him she loved him an' wanted to be his. Cú thought the woman played some kind o' trick on him, so he rejected her by saying he did not have the time."

Aveline shook her head. "Poor woman."

"Not so much." He wiped the water from his chin onto the back of his hand and walked over to the plaid. "Hurt by his rejection, she told him she would come in three forms when he was in battle. In each guise she would try to take his concentration by harming him. Do you want to know how he replied?"

Mr. O'Devlin sat near her.

She felt the heat emanating off him and his close proximity prevented her from forming intelligible words. "Oh...yes. Very much so."

"Cú told Morrighán each time he would also stop her with harm an' the only way to recover was through his blessing, which he would not give her. She came to him in battle as a she-wolf, a water creature, an' a cow as she foretold, only to end up harmed by the man instead.

"After he fought the war, Cú walked along the road until he found an old woman with a cow. Being thirsty, he asked the woman for a drink o' the cow's milk. Morríghan gave him a glass, and in return he blessed her for the offering. He healed her after all."

Aveline did not want the story to end. She needed to hear more of his musical voice. "Did they end up together?"

He shook his head. "*Ní.*" His answer was too short, but it was in Gaelic.

Her head felt lighter. "Whatever happened to them?"

He shrugged. "Cú died in the next battle. Morríghan held him in her arms as he passed. She turned into a crow right after, perched upon his shoulder, and guarded over the body. 'Tis the reason why she continues to walk alone on the moors. Her sadness surrounds her for eternity."

A tear threatened to fall down Aveline's cheek. "Such a tragedy." Unable to gauge his reaction, she said, "Nonetheless, Mr. O'Devlin, quite a lovely story. Thank you very much for sharing it."

Aveline thought she would incorporate a

similar one into the book she was writing.

He arose from the blanket and straightened his wrinkled garb. "Right, I believe 'tis time to get back to work. There are still a few hours left before supper. I am sure we can find something to do on the farm." Grabbing his jacket from the ground, he took the wicker basket and pulled the flaps down to conceal the opening. A red ribbon tied at the top prevented the items inside from falling out.

Aveline refastened her bonnet, took his proffered hand to assist her from the blanket, and allowed him to draw her into his waiting arms. He dropped the basket, and she was swept into his embrace. Then she felt his lips on hers.

She loved the feel of his calloused hand as it caressed the side of her cheek. She placed her arms around his neck and felt his warm skin.

He smelled like soap and the soft scent of

the leaves the surrounding breeze carried.

Separating from the kiss was difficult, but done with great care. She gave him one last glance. Her cheeks felt hot, but the sun was not to blame this time.

👑 👑 👑

Ciarán pulled his eyes from hers as he shook the plaid and placed it in the crook of his arm. He took the wicker basket into the same hand and offered his free arm to her. She immediately locked elbows with him. He smelled lavender in the air.

She tantalized him without saying a word.

He turned to look at her, as they stopped in front of the barn. "A good day to you, Lady Aveline. I enjoyed the outing. We shall definitely do it again."

She stood there, waiting. He wondered if she was hoping he'd kiss her once more. As much as he wished to embrace her a third time, he needed to maintain control over the situation and guard his heart. That meant keeping his distance.

He grasped her right hand and placed a chaste kiss on its back.

He knew he could pass for a rich country gentleman. Unfortunately, his dimpled smile inevitably gave him away as Ciarán O'Devlin, the true manager of a farm in Northern Ireland. But now his heart belonged to a woman.

Chapter 10

*H*e was a stubborn Irishman indeed, Aveline thought.

Despite their closeness, he seemed determined to keep his distance. Mr. O'Devlin never looked up from his work and bowed his head each time he walked by. She would not allow him to distract her further from completing her day's chores, and she wheeled the barrow out onto the field.

Mr. MacRory forked hay into a pile. He acknowledged her when she walked near.

"Good afternoon to you, Lady Aveline."

She nodded. "The same to you."

She walked into the barley field and inspected the plants. Did they grow two inches in three hours or was she imagining it? No, she was not imagining the growth. There were weeds everywhere. She'd neglected her duties long enough for the wild plants to sprout!

Aveline thought back to before the picnic. What was she doing? Mr. O'Devlin and Mr. MacRory showed her how to feed the chickens and milk the goats, while the brothers checked the vegetables. The nerve of the Irishman to distract her. Before asking her to join him by the river, he kept her busy with other chores, and she'd allowed him to.

Does the man already own my heart? She asked herself, knowing she wouldn't receive an answer.

She procrastinated overlong with her thoughts. If she did not start working, she would look out into the distant fields and her mind would become lost again. She bent down and dug her hands into the rich dirt. Under the surface, the soil was cool and moist. The first root in her grasp, she pulled as hard as she could, easily freed the obstruction from the soil, and moved onto the next one. The blisters on her hands hadn't the time to heal and they pained each time she pulled too hard.

She threw the weed into the wheelbarrow and continued to the next plant.

She did not know how she would get through the day, knowing Mr. O'Devlin worked in the distance, and she wasn't able to see him.

Although Aveline felt she could not last without another kiss from him, all she currently wanted was for him to smile in her direction.

His smile could brighten the rest of her days and warm the rest of her nights.

👑 👑 👑

When supper ended, Aveline undressed and took up her quill to write.

After the wedding, Blythe and Vincent had a singular marriage. He traveled elsewhere to his many estates and continued on with his business. No doubt out of regret. All the while, she managed the household.

They married out of necessity and she desperately wanted Vincent to show her some affection.

Three months earlier, Blythe happened to stumble into his arms while cleaning his bedchamber. Vincent couldn't stop with just a kiss. He held enough morals to marry her after he'd compromised her. Without him around, something went missing from her life.

She expected him back that same evening and she wanted to discuss the matter with him during supper.

His mood was stable when he walked through the door. She watched as he hung his frock silently upon the peg. She went down into a low curtsy and he bowed back to her in an aloof manner.

He announced to the room, not particularly looking in her direction. "My lady wife, I am in hunger, let us dine early tonight."

With her head bowed, Blythe took her usual seat near the table's head, as Vincent took his. They were served a steaming silver tray full of potato soup, steamed fish, and vegetables in sauce. He planned the premature meal without consulting her. As mistress of the house, she was required to make all dinner preparations. She decided to speak, lest silence ensued further. "Enjoying your meal, my lord?"

"Yes, of course, Cook is the best in the whole county." He did not inquire about her taste.

"You always say those words, it seems."

He looked up, but did not make eye contact. "Whatever do you mean by such a statement?"

She sighed. "Well, we never partake in conversation, my lord. I fear you do not really care for me."

Vincent held his fork in midair. "If I did not care for you, you certainly would not have the protection of my name."

"Is your name the only part of this marriage that matters to you?"

He wiped his mouth with the cloth. "Most certainly not, madam!"

She forked the food on her plate,

unable to eat a single pea.

"Then, what would you say if I told you I feel deep affection for you?"

He ate fast. "I would be flattered and tell you I would feel the same, if only I had the time."

She sipped wine. "You could make time for me. The estate is so lonely when you are not here."

"You know of the duties I'm required to perform in accordance to my title. We discussed this before marriage."

Unfortunately, he did not notice her loss of appetite.

The time was now or never to tell him.

"Yes, I do believe we did, but what if I told you I desired more than just your name?"

"What else more do you need? You are the mistress of a beautiful home.

You have all the dresses you may ever desire. You have food, and servants to do all of your work, yet you still act like a maid. Do you forget in what further position you would have been in if it was not for my kindness toward you?" His intense gaze bored into her. "If such information does not make you happy, then I have not a clue what will." He ate again, devouring the meal like a hungry lion.

"I am with child, sir." She winced, expecting him to explode with the news. He looked up and wiped his mouth upon the linen cloth again, as she held her breath for his imminent reaction.

Vincent hadn't prepared for the possibility his pretty young wife would

drill him about his feelings. Especially so soon after his arrival to the manse. Now her reasons for doing so made sense.

He felt his features soften. "Do you speak true, madam?" He never forgot his strong affection for her.

Ever since his father died and left him the title, he had cared for his poor ailing mother, alone. His temper flared ever so often. The few servants who remained left the household. They claimed he'd gone mad and refused to work for him any longer. He was given the chore of hiring a whole new house staff, and decided never to open his heart to anyone again.

Knowing he could get an heir, gave him determination to become a better person than his father. A man who chose a mistress over his own wife. With genuine concern etching his face, he inquired, "How are you feeling...Blythe?"

She lifted her head and noticed a slight smile brighten his features. Her name on his lips sounded new, even welcoming. "Well, I could be better," Blythe told him somberly.

A knock upon the door startled Aveline from her writing.

She reluctantly separated from her work, and slipped on the green dress she had worn the previous day. She opened the door a crack to see who disturbed her. Mr. O'Devlin's winsome smile reached her long before she could smell the fresh scent of soap on his skin.

His voice's lilt held a beckoning tone, as his eyes leveled on her face. "You must get dressed, *cailín*, I want to take you somewhere."

So, he did wish to see and talk to her again after all.

"At this hour of the night, Mr. O'Devlin? Are you sure whatever you wish to show me cannot wait until tomorrow? You never know what—" Aveline wanted to continue writing, while ideas were fresh in her mind.

His shoulder prevented the door from closing further. "No, it cannot wait. You will only receive the full effect o' the experience if you are there at night."

His smile convinced her to set out. "Well, I shall not be the one to miss such an experience. I will meet you downstairs momentarily." She reluctantly pushed the door closed.

The longing to write more weighed upon Aveline's chest. The story had become a major part of her life over the last couple of weeks and she was hard-pressed to separate herself from such a close friend. With one last look at the paper stacked on her desk, she grabbed her brown shawl and left the chamber.

She knew the stubborn man waited for her at the front door.

She did not wish to keep him waiting long, lest he change his mind and never speak to her again.

Chapter 11

At Mr. O'Devlin's bidding, Aveline climbed beside him in the buggy stopped outside the door. Two horses were harnessed up and their breathing clouded in the cool night breeze. He took up the reins in the moonlight and hiked the horses to a fast trot toward the main dirt road. A marker saying, "Carrickmore," pointed in their direction.

She held her bonnet, as the cold wind whipped through her clothing. "I would much appreciate if you told me where we are going." She turned her head toward the man who drove with such a natural sense of ease. His hands held the reins in an iron grip. She longed to feel his hard and masculine embrace and imagined his arms enfolding her when they kissed.

He glanced over at her then turned his head back to the road. "Trust me, you will enjoy the outing."

She knew her face displayed how much trust she gave him, because she could feel her heart shining in her eyes. Unfortunately, she knew he could not discern the look from any other, so her feelings remained unseen.

👑 👑 👑

The buggy stopped. The half-hour drive had passed too quickly. "We are here, Lady Aveline." He looked at the old wooden structure with familiarity.

The pub's crooked sign, which read *O'Malley's* in engraved letters, creaked, swinging back and forth on rusted hinges.

Ciarán noticed the frown she wore and braced himself for her negative comments about the pub's rundown exterior. "You cannot judge anything by the outside. I am sure you will love the inside once we enter."

She nodded.

He parked the buggy in the rear and exited. She took his hand as he helped her down. Walking around to the pub's front, he followed her through the door.

He'd known the pub for years and the place had once played a major part in his life. The cultural pull was intense and he wanted her to embrace the surroundings with open arms. After all, he was beside her. If she embraced him too, he would not complain.

The high noise level hit Ciarán's ears and he knew they'd come in time for music. The wooden tables and bar across the room overflowed with patrons. The interior wooden beams were polished to a nice sheen, and many ancient decorations covered the walls. Some resembled painted portraits, while others were Celtic in origin and were handcrafted.

A man sat on an oak bar stool and yelled for a pint. Another man on the opposite side of the room yelled in Gaelic for a whiskey dram.

Ciarán glanced at Aveline, then frowned, and looked around the room. Everyone stared at her as she walked into the pub. Although he knew they were foxed, his possessive nature was on guard until they found a seat.

Aveline leaned close and whispered in an angry tone. "Why on Earth would you ever bring me to a place such as this, Mr. O'Devlin? They must not know staring is rude, because everyone cannot get their eyes off me."

He chuckled, and felt pleasure run through him. "Yes, now I am assured o' the fact you are most certainly a *cailín dathúil*." He ordered them both a pint of ale, as he placed her in an empty chair by the bar. He liked masking his compliments in Gaelic. Luckily, she loved hearing his people's language and her ignorance of the meaning spawned her appreciation.

But she disregarded his statement and looked at the mug with disgust.

He encouraged her to take a sip. "Well, surely the brew won't drink itself. Just take a swig." Then he gave her his dimpled smile and hoped she would give in.

She picked up the foaming brew. "If I do not like it, will you forgive me?"

"O' course, *cailín*." He hid another smile as she drank a sip and sputtered. All first timers drank the foam, and she was no exception. He cursed the possibility she'd cease drinking based on the foam's taste.

"This drink is absolutely revolting, Mr. O'Devlin!" she said loudly.

The barmaid became overly curious as to the woman's identity and looked in their direction. A new face in the pub always peaked Molly McGinnis's interest.

Her sudden curiosity in the Englishwoman encouraged Ciarán to ignore her watchful eyes. "You only drank foam, Lady Aveline. If you will just sip like I do, dipping ya mouth into the foam, you will get the drink to come from under." He demonstrated with a large sip of the dark brew.

She tried after him with more success, and finished the glass, enjoying the rich malt barley taste.

He finished with his mug long before she finished half of hers, but he patiently waited before he ordered another round.

She drank the last sip with a smile and he called to the barmaid. "'Twill be another round for us, Molly!" He flashed his winning grin, happy to see Aveline enjoying his culture. He knew she was an integral part of his future, not only because she owned the farm, but because his emotions for her were increasing.

"Comin' right up, O'Devlin." The bar maid said, as she poured the dark liquid into their mugs from a tap in a wooden barrel.

Then just for his ears alone, after setting the drinks in front of the couple, Molly said in Gaelic, "You know, if you wanted to ditch the colleen you have, we could have a right fine time upstairs like the good old days." Her bosom popped out ever so much, as she leaned over the bar.

Aveline quickly drank the ale, hoping to drown out their words with the incoming dizziness. She knew they talked about her. Not only did the barmaid gesture in her direction, but she also cocked her head toward Mr. O'Devlin and then the upstairs.

Mr. O'Devlin's response in Gaelic sounded more musical than before.

The barmaid sucked in her breath and strained to get her next words out. The word *sasanach* was in the woman's speech.

What were they saying?

There was raw emotion in his words. *Especially when I am involved. I heard you mention my last name, Irishman.*

A saucy smile came upon the barmaid's lips.

Before Aveline could keep up with the speech, Mr. O'Devlin's tone indicated he was no longer in a good mood. After speaking, he gulped all the ale from his mug.

The barmaid sighed. She moved away from them, rubbing her hands on her soiled apron and proceeded to help another patron who walked into the door.

What were they saying to make

O'Devlin's hand shake his mug in anger? Aveline tried to push the question away as she was handed another pint. She felt light-headed from the alcohol. After all, she was on her third one.

👑 👑 👑

Molly's words affected Ciarán so much so he gulped his ale too fast. His head started to spin. He would tell Aveline the bad news himself - the truth about his past. She would find out his secrets sooner or later. The bar-maid was right.

Their friendship required honesty and re-spect. As he turned toward her for the con-fession, a quintet of men with instruments walked into the pub. The music had arrived.

She watched the band. "They are playing instruments I've never seen before. Can you tell me what they are called, Mr. O'Devlin?"

Ciarán's smile returned. "The one there,

me dear, is a fiddle." He pointed to the far right, and moved down the line. "The weird and wonderful contraption with the pipes is called the *Uilleann*. Next, is the flute, a *Bodhrán agus* Bones, an' last there is a hornpipe. The group is called a *ceilí* band."

He awaited her reaction to the beautiful music. He was annoyed at the interruption, but music was the reason he brought her to the pub.

He hoped she enjoyed it as much as he did. The musicians played a jig, or *port*. Any minute, the patrons would start dancing.

His temper disappeared with her radiant smile.

Her eyes remained glued to the other men. "The music is brilliant, Mr. O'Devlin."

He knew she meant every word. He needed to spend as much time with her as he could. "Care to have a dance with me, Lady Aveline?"

"I do not know how to do the Celtic

dance—I would only embarrass you if I tried."

She set an empty glass down upon the table, her cheeks flushed as she hinted toward another round for them.

Chapter 12

Ciarán gestured with his head, his dark hair moving ever so slightly. "'Tis as good a time to learn a *port* as any. Besides, I'm afraid there will be no ale left for anyone else. Give it a try an' come with me."

High spirits were renewed as he rose from his stool and took Aveline's hand. Maybe he should not tell her anything about himself. His past could wait another hour or more.

He led her to the dance floor. A few pub guests danced in single *port*s.

He took both her hands leaving only enough distance between them to perform the dance. "First, point ya right toe out in front of you, straight out from ya knee, like this."

She tried the move, but before lifting her leg to straighten her foot, she nearly stumbled to the ground. If not for his strong but gentle grip upon her hands, she would've fallen in front of everyone.

The few drinks she consumed placed a sparkle in her eyes, and he chuckled knowing she was well seasoned from so little drink. After balancing, she tried the dance a second time and succeeded. The *port* came natural to her.

"'Tis a grand job you did, *cailín*. Next, step with ya right foot an' bring ya left foot behind the first." He watched her try the move and almost fall over again. He held her steady. "You are trying too hard, really. Just take a breather an' then do the step. You can count one-two, if you need."

Molly glanced over at them, apparently holding in her laughter.

He gave the barmaid a frown and she returned to helping her eager patrons without another glance. Turning back to Aveline, he saw she was able to do what he taught her without wobbling. "Now 'tis time to move ya toe to meet ya left knee an' then you just give a little hop."

This action made her giggle. "You're very nimble, Mr. O'Devlin. I daresay it may take hours before I ever learn this dance."

"Me people learned a lot from the fairy folk you know, an' this is one o' me favorites." He heard her sweet little laugh again, causing his heart to beat faster and a smile to cross his lips. "You try."

She danced so well.

Of course, she was a good dancer. He

knew she danced all the time in England. Her father mentioned balls often. Ciarán wanted her to appreciate the *port* as much as the...what do they call it? The walls? *No, the demmed waltz.*

Her feet did not stop moving. "I believe the *port* is getting easier the more I practice."

He closed his eyes at the smell of her hair as the curls went up and down with the movement. "Right, those words sound wonderful to me ears, Lady Aveline." He really disliked calling her "Lady." The words sounded too formal. Just "Aveline" would sound much better on his lips, but he knew she would not appreciate him only using her Christian name in public without permission.

"This will sound strange, but all you have to do for the next step is bend ya right leg to the back, with ya foot out. Just use ya left foot to hop in place."

The step made her topple again. An action she could not prevent.

He held out his arm, as it tensed in readiness to steady her fall, and waited until she was stable enough to complete the steps. "The rest o' it comes to you with the music." He showed her the last part and repeated the step.

Her effort astounded him. He dropped one of her hands, holding one still out as she twirled around him doing her own version of the dance.

They poured laughter and vitality into every move they made, until the music stopped and the musicians took their bows.

Ciarán saw Molly glance toward them again. She made him uneasy, and Aveline needed to return to her bed and sleep off the drink.

👑 👑 👑

They walked to the bar to collect his coat and her wrap, proceeding to take out the coin to pay for their drinks. Molly approached, and with a smirk, whispered in English. "No need ta worry about the coin, Mr. O'Devlin. You know where ta come ta pay me back. It was right fine meeting ya new landlord as it was." She turned to Aveline. "Me name's Molly McGinnis."

Did O'Devlin have a history with her? Aveline's curiosity would not relent. *Was he still spending time with the barmaid?*

Then a new wave of questions hit her. *Why would Miss McGinnis offer to give him drinks for free? Surely, he could pay his bill with the funds he made from the farm. Unless...no, Mr. O'Devlin is not that kind of man. Or is he?*

She did not know much about the Irishman after all.

"My name's Aveline Peyton. It is a pleasure meeting you," she said matter-of-factly, gaining her superiority over the other woman. Her dignity was all she had left.

Chapter 13

Ciarán drove the buggy toward the farm.

Not a word passed between them, until the very inebriated Aveline asked, "Why did Molly offer to pay your tab?"

If he did not answer her right away she would have no trouble finding out the details from the barmaid. "'Tis true I am completely bereft of coin. As to the details, I promised me brothers I would never tell a soul." Although not angry, he was distressed. He wanted to broach the subject in his own time. Not when she'd forget everything he said in the morning.

A sad look clouded her face. "Please tell me. I long to know as much as I can about you." The ride home lasted longer than expected. She affected him. "The concern you have for me is nothing less than genuine, I'm sure," he said.

"But it is."

He could not resist telling her the truth based on the sorrow in her voice. "If only I'd enough time to tell you the whole truth about me."

She smiled, encouraging his speech. "I'm glad you trust me enough to tell me such delicate information. There is enough time."

His eyes remained on the dirt road. "Right, I will tell you as much as I can, but no one is to know I told you." He pulled on the reins to make the horse slow down. "Me brothers got themselves in a bit o' debt in the workhouse. Every night a boxing competition took place. You've heard o' boxing where you come from, *cailín,* right?"

Her attention was captured. "No. I daresay what is it?"

Ciarán steered the buggy off the road and placed the reins in his lap. "Well, 'tis a very unladylike sport, involving a bit o' hitting with ya hands. Like this." He balled his fists in front of her and did a jab at the wind. He flexed each muscle underneath his tweed jacket with the movement. "'Tis a popular thing to do when the day ended. The workers would bet who'd win each night an' me brothers bet on themselves. Soon they reaped rewards, which became a hefty amount I might say."

"What was the amount?"

He had been afraid she would ask. He gave her the only comparison she would understand. "Enough to buy a large estate an' pay for many servants." *Something he had never experienced in his whole life.*

Ciarán did not care for wealth. So why did he feel distressed every time he compared his station to the Englishwoman's?

Her words were hushed. "How did they lose all the money?"

The shadow on his face dissipated. "One night, a new challenger came to face them alone. Seán O'Rooney. He was bigger than both o' them combined. Eònan an' Sòlas gambled everything they'd earned an' more that they would defeat this man."

He laughed. "They were too stubborn to admit they'd lose an', guess what?" He did not give her time to ask before he spoke. "The large man seized every bit o' their earnings in the workhouse, along with their clothing, their food, everything. He wanted more coin, so he chased after them, until they fled to me town.

"Eónan appeared in the pub looking for me while Sólas searched for a place to stay the night. I let them work on the farm to pay me back after I promised the large man all me earnings for the next five years."

☙ ☙ ☙

Five years' worth of pay? I daresay he is mad for offering such an amount. "Surely you knew they brought themselves into such a mess. You did not have to make the business of getting them out yourself."

He scowled. "The man threatened to kill me own brothers. You would've done the same for ya family."

An image of her late parent's came into mind and almost caused her tears, but she prevented the waterfall with a reply. "If what you say is true, then you—then you—" She lost her words in a stutter. What could she possibly blame him for?

"I mean every word I say, *cailín*."

She could no longer remain poised on the

hard wooden seat and stood. "From how I view the situation, you spent every coin you earned and ever will earn from the farm paying off those...those bets! Mr. O'Devlin, that is completely careless of you and—"

"No, I am not careless an' 'tis wrong of you to accuse me." *But those words condemn me as a liar.*

She saw the tic in his jaw and knew she should not argue with him any longer. But she needed to voice her concerns. "Just think of all the people who depend on your income. How are you going to be able to pay them?"

His eyes met hers. "After knowing each other only for a few weeks, you stand here an' call me out!"

Ciarán gathered the reins and refrained from looking in her direction. He adjusted his flat cap and stood in silence until Aveline spoke again.

She needed to free her mind. "So you did

waste your wages on bets? How do you pay Miss O'Grace and the rest of the workers? Molly? I am sure you've spent every night with her upstairs just to get a pint of ale every day." The thought nearly made her faint. Aveline tried to remain calm, despite the rising blush upon her cheeks. She'd never been this forward with a man in her life.

"You perceive me wrong, *cailín*." His voice became a whisper. "I spent all those nights terribly alone an' desiring someone like you to come along an' bind me with her voice." His eyes closed and reopened. "If you would let me explain further, I do care about everyone who works on me farm. I only promised me wages to O'Rooney. So for the past four years, I've divided the profits for everyone, but meself an' those *punts* go straight to him."

Her combined sadness and regret, encouraged his features to soften. "Is this the whole truth, Mr. O'Devlin?"

"Yes...I speak truly. Allow me to reiterate me point a bit more." His lips were upon hers before she blinked. How could she refuse to believe him any longer when he kissed her so thoroughly?

She hardly remembered when he stopped the buggy a good ways into their conversation. "Point taken." Aveline reluctantly separated from the kiss, smoothed her skirts, and adjusted her bonnet. They reseated themselves and he drove them the rest of the way to the farmhouse, stopping the buggy in the drive. "You must be exhausted. I know I am. The hour waxes late, we have a long day to face on the farm tomorrow."

He helped her from the seat. She fell into his embrace, his encompassing arms held her close to him, as he gave her another quick minute of Heaven.

Smoothing back the curls from her face, he kissed her thoroughly before opening the door. "Ya father taught me well. Please don't underestimate me true intentions for the farm, *cailín*." He winked. "The consequences would not be so pleasant the next time. Sweet dreams."

She nodded. "Thank you for telling me. Good night, Mr. O'Devlin." He closed the door for her and she heard his quick footsteps down the porch steps.

She was too exhausted to write and retired. *A very trying night indeed,* Aveline thought, as she lay in bed. *If only he would talk to me more often.* His face was the last image in her mind before falling asleep.

Chapter 14

Aveline paced the small living room, trying to remain calm. She didn't like how Mr. O'Devlin had become cold and distant before the upcoming farmer's market trip in two weeks. His behavior caused unwelcome tension between them. Every time they became closer, he would give her reasons why they should remain apart. He mentioned too many times how she was born into her station and how he had spent his whole life earning his. Her father most certainly did not marry her mother for money. She knew Mr. O'Devlin was a poor Irish farmer, and a union with him would go against the English Crown, but nothing would deter her feelings.

She always followed her heart. Her heart took her to Ireland, upon her father's wishes, and there she was introduced to the Irishman. Surely, her father knew she would meet him.

Mr. O'Devlin's accusing words echoed in the room. "Women don't know anything about running a farm. The workers don't like someone watching every move they make, Lady Aveline." He sat in a small cushioned armchair, talking to the fireplace wall, while drinking from a pint. He refused to look in her direction.

She looked at her bandaged hands and folded them into fists. Mr. O'Devlin and she went from making love to arguing within a few days' time, and she didn't understand how his feelings could change so abruptly.

"I am trying to learn as much as I can about farming. I've made steady progress. The crops I watched over for the past month and a half have grown wonderfully. Observing is the only way I can learn." Aveline wanted to tear the thin material from her hands and show him how she could work against the pain. "You specifically gave me instruction to learn through other means, did you not?"

His eyes flickered to her hands. "Well, yes..."

♔ ♔ ♔

A week after their outing to the pub, Mr. O'Devlin discovered the bandages on her hands. He overheard her conversation with Mr. MacRory.

She smiled. The day was bright and sunny. "How are you today?"

The Scotsman walked beside her. "Very

well, lass. How about ya self? Hands feelin' any better?"

Aveline lifted the appendages for a closer inspection. "Very much so. Thank you for the insight. Without you, I could not remain on the fields." If only words could express her gratitude.

"'Tis no matter..." He stalled his speech when Mr. O'Devlin walked closer.

She didn't have time to hide her hands.

Surely, the Irishman had heard every word. "Come, I must speak to you in private, Lady Aveline."

She followed him into the barn.

Then, he turned. "What is the matter? Are those bindings on ya hands?"

She knew he was more concerned for the farm than her. "No need to worry about me, Mr. O'Devlin. The linen is a fix for a temporary quandary. I assure you, my duties will not become affected in the least."

His eyes changed. They turned misty, almost opaque. "Ya duty, Lady Aveline, is not to work on this farm. Any other landowner would live in leisure, while everyone under him worked themselves 'til death."

Aveline mocked him. "I am not one of *those* landowners, Mr. O'Devlin."

"Be it as it may." He sighed, resting his shoulder on a wooden beam. "You should take a break. Let MacRory prepare the barley."

She could not believe her ears. "A break?"

"Yes, take some time for ya writing, or whichever else puts you at ease." His voice lowered. "I don't wish to see you in pain any longer."

She'd been working despite the pain for so long. The throbbing never affected Aveline until now. "I do want to finish my novel..."

A smile alighted on his face.

She was a besotted fool indeed. "I

daresay time off will heal my wounds, but do not expect me to be away for very long. I want to reap what I sow, Mr. O'Devlin."

"Very well, then. Shall we make our way to luncheon before the food grows cold?" He opened the barn door for her.

She was sorry to step out. Life could change so much in a few minutes. To think, a few minutes did change everything. Her decision to reenter the field after luncheon caused Mr. O'Devlin's temper to flare and he requested her immediate presence in the living room.

👑 👑 👑

Aveline glared at the Irishman. How dare he treat demand that she do his bidding! She pointed to the door before crossing her arms. "If you have an issue with the way I run things, then you can find a more suitable place to live and work." Her world would crumble if he left. Her heart would never allow her to sing again. "In which I am sure, Mr. O'Devlin, you have naught anywhere else to go. My father would roll over in his grave if he found I was residing with a man whilst unmarried. Nonetheless, a poor Irishman. At the least, we are not under society's nose being in a small town out in the country." She paused to stare at him with a pointed look.

Why did her heart betray her and beat faster at the sight of him?

He smiled. "You mean ya society's nose, *cailín*?" He put the mug to his lips. His chest heaved with unspent laughter.

She could not believe he'd laugh during a serious conversation.

His Gaelic would not sway her words this time. "You are one to speak such nonsense. When I first arrived, I did not receive kindness from anyone. Mr. MacRory and Miss O'Grace were the only exceptions, but they offered to help because they pitied me. I cannot believe I'm still treated unkindly by the one person my father would've moved mountains for."

Aveline paused and took a deep breath. She held back a verbal tidal wave. Her words became hushed. "I've not done a single harm to any of your people since I've been here, but no one seems to care a single whit about that. All everyone can do is laugh and call me *sasanach*, while the one person I care about most does not even speak to me at all. There comes a time, Mr. O'Devlin, when a lady has quite enough ill treatment to put her over the edge. I've reached a point where I am left in complete frustration and with nothing else to say."

She sighed and plopped herself down upon the settee across from him. Maybe she should pretend to swoon like the ladies in her country when they sought attention from a man.

No matter how many times she fainted, the Irishman still would not notice her. Hopefully, he would not laugh at her again.

O'Devlin's eyes widened as he looked in her direction. She didn't have to swoon after all. "You've much fire in you, Lady Aveline. There is goodness in you, but not enough to stir the Irish people, especially me brothers. The English took much from them. They lost their ancestral home to ya father, an' many relatives continue to lose their lives retaliating ya ways." He rose from the chair with his mug and walked toward the staircase. "Not everyone was as lucky to have the educational opportunities I was given. If you will be as kind as to excuse me, I am departing to me room until supper is ready. Good evening." He tipped his head.

This was how he responded to everything she said? He would drown his sorrows in ale, all alone in his room? Indeed he was *insufferable*!

Aveline heard the floorboards creak as his footsteps ascended the stairs and into his bedroom. She would not allow him to escape her this time. With every argument, he would either walk away or have the last word. *Or the last delightful kiss.* She vowed never again to stand behind, while he blew off his steam alone.

Her affections for him did not prevent her from following, and soon she knocked upon the door he hid behind.

Ciarán didn't know how to respond to a woman's frustration. The passion that poured forth from her mouth affected him. He needed to escape before he vowed to do everything in his power to make her happy. His room was the best refuge he could find.

Sitting on his bed, he concluded that a poor Irish farmer could never make her happy. She was not a woman who should work on a farm. Her soft hands were cut, blistered, and bleeding, yet, she continued working. She was sensible, strong, and honest. She deserved someone who shared those characteristics and who possessed enough coin to keep her from hard work. But, he lacked that wealth.

He did not have a single shilling left to his name. She was right. Her society would never allow them to be together.

A knock sounded on the door.

He opened it. The fire-haired beauty entered the room. He knew nothing could interrupt such an earth-shattering moment in time. When he looked back on everyone who said they knew what love felt like, he realized their words would never describe the way his body felt when she was near. He retreated to the room's far side with his back to her.

A happy wave crashed through his body,

and he fought back tears. Without her, he would become an empty shell. A hand came up to wipe his eyes from the flood. He heard her walk in and close the door, knowing she left the latch unlocked.

Her words sounded strained and forlorn. "What can I do, Mr. O'Devlin...to have your brothers like me? To have Mr. MacRory and Miss O'Grace not pity me?" She paused. "Please, tell me what I've done on this farm to have you detest me so? Am I not like my father after all, then? Am I worse?"

Ciarán did not respond to her interrogations. The questions cut like a knife through his resolve.

He tried so hard not to become attached, but he wanted more than anything to comfort her. Without hesitation, he turned and strode closer. "You are very kind like ya father, Lady Aveline..." He grazed a hand over her cheek.

She placed her hand over his. "I wish you would call me Aveline."

Her name was beautiful. "This is what you've done wrong, Aveline." Placing both arms around her neck, he embraced her. Moments passed before she encircled him in her arms. But he did not kiss her.

Instead, he held her close.

Miss O'Grace adored her. MacRory liked her, maybe loved her. Even Éonan and Solás admired her. Knowing all this would give her the satisfaction she so longed for. The information however, wouldn't change anything. He could never spend his life with her. At least these few moments still remained.

Aveline's sharp intake of breath encouraged him to venture his hands lower onto her waist.

She murmured. "I do not understand why this is wrong, Mr. O'Devlin."

"My name is Ciarán, Aveline. I would much prefer you to call me that." He moved his lips down to kiss lightly upon her neck. "'Tis better if you stop worrying altogether an' relax." Her skin was soft, warm...

She flinched from his touch. "We've not known each other very long. There is a lot we have to learn about one another. Are you sure we should become so familiar without..." A moan interrupted her speech.

He smiled in satisfaction. "Yes, is this not what you've wanted, too? I'm afraid the attraction between us is hard to resist. Ever since we shared a kiss that day in the field, I cannot resist doing so again and again." He kissed along her arm, and then went to her mouth. He used his tongue to part her lips, then he drew back after a moment. "You always keep me coming back for more."

Their rhythm continued until they were about to lower themselves upon the welcoming bed.

A knock came upon the door.

He cursed at the maid's inopportune tim-

163

ing. "Mr. O'Devlin, supper be on the table. 'Tis a surprise to me you've not made ya way downstairs ta eat. You always be the first one at the table. I 'ave not seen Lady Aveline either, as ta her whereabouts..."

The couple immediately split and fixed their clothing as the woman let herself in.

Miss O'Grace smirked.

Ciarán gave her a scowl.

"I see you're otherwise occupied. Please do not allow me ta interrupt." Scurrying from the room with a giggle, she closed the door.

He muttered another oath under his breath, as he turned to Aveline. "Right, well we must go to supper, before anything else seems remiss around here. We will continue this at another time, *cailín*." He gave her a dimpled smile and quit the room.

Ciarán did not believe there would ever come another time.

Chapter 15

As Aveline searched for Mr. MacRory near the barn, he walked past her on the way to his cottage.

The night stood quiet, except for the slumbering animals. She was on a mission to clear her mind, and drive Ciarán from it, so she could focus on making profits from the farm.

Ironically, the way she had chosen to clear her head could just as likely have the opposite effect.

She walked toward the Scotsman, who leaned on a beam watching her approach. "Mr. MacRory, would you drive me to O'Malley's? I need to have a drink."

His laughter rolled through him like thunder as he studied her. The sound resonated in the quiet darkness. "I dinnae think 'tis a grand idea, Lady Aveline, for you ta be seen in the place all alone. The lads in town dinnae take kindly ta English strangers in their pub."

She gave him a pointed look. "Molly knows me. Ciar...Mr. O'Devlin took me to the pub before. Surely, it's not a problem as long as she's around."

He placed a hand on his bearded chin. "I couldna argue with you, unless I want me ears boxed. Let us be on then." He bade her to follow him, and after he harnessed the horse, they climbed into the buggy.

They didn't speak along the way. All she could think about was why he agreed so readily to drive her. Did he find it amusing that an Englishwoman wanted a drink?

Soon he stopped the buggy in the front of the pub.

"Thank you so much. I will not forget the kindness you've showed me this past month," she said.

He chuckled as she exited the buggy. "I will be back ta get you in two hours. Make sure you are able ta walk when you leave or O'Devlin will suspect where you've been."

Aveline hoped he wouldn't tell Ciarán. The Irishman would come and cause a scene.

She heard beautiful music playing as she sauntered through the pub's doors and took a seat at the bar. Without Ciarán, the tavern seemed lonelier than she remembered. Why should she worry over his absence?

He had been very unpleasant these past few days. To think the man would resort to outright seduction to avoid telling her his true feelings. She desired to drown his face from her mind with a few pints of poison.

Molly's amusement shown in her smirk. "Good evening ta you, Lady Aveline. Where be ya lad tonight?"

She had obviously surprised the barmaid when she arrived without an escort, but she was most certainly not tied to anyone. "I do not know, nor does it concern me where he is. The man is a beguiling devil."

Molly sighed. "That he is, but most men are, I s'pose."

Aveline thought every woman likely fell for Ciarán's smile.

The barmaid seemed to be no exception. "None o' this nonsense tonight. What kind o' drink would you be wantin' ta try?"

"I want something I can drown my sorrows in." She considered unrequited love the greatest sorrow a person can feel. She'd give up her rights to her father's English estates to be with the man she loved.

Molly pulled an elongated bottle from the

cupboard. "I believe I've just the thing for you." She blew the dust from the label and poured half the contents into a decanter and then a little into a small glass. "Try this, me girl. 'Tis sure ta singe the hair right off ya head. Just whiff before you taste."

Aveline touched her head. "I hope that is not the case, I'm fond of my hair." She lifted the glass, sniffed the contents, poured the liquid down her throat...and gagged. But she refused to sputter the liquid all over, so she clamped her lips together and swallowed the fire.

Molly laughed.

The alcohol burned all the way down, and a sheath of goose bumps covered Aveline's body when it hit her system. She compared the taste to drinking from a murky bog and felt her mind floating away with the mist. Despite its taste, the sensation it left was quite adequate for her current mood. "Another."

The barmaid laughed again and poured more into her glass. "I'm going ta leave you with the decanter. You may drink as much o' it as you like," Molly said and waited for her response.

Aveline lifted the glass for a second time. "What is it, may I ask?"

"'Tis the finest Irish Whiskey on this side o' the *inis*. The bottle is nigh ten an' eight years old." With those words, the barmaid left to assist another eager patron.

Aveline gulped down the glass's contents. Ciarán's image remained blurred in her mind. Looking around the room, she noticed a few men staring at her from a dark corner. Apprehension clawed its way through the fog and skittered up her spine. She might not see well at the moment, but she sensed danger.

She tried to find Molly, but the woman had disappeared. Aveline turned her attention back to the glass she held.

Ignoring the strange feeling as a mind

trick, she poured more whiskey.

She heard a man approaching in quick strides and watched him sit in the vacant stool beside her. His thick sideburns jutted from underneath the flat cap he wore sideways. "What you be drinkin' there, lass?" The man's clothes were torn and gray. He spoke with a deep voice and he was tall and wide. Quite frankly, he could scare anyone.

She emptied the glass again and felt very dizzy. "Only the finessh Irish Whiskey," she snapped, hoping if she responded curtly, the man would leave.

"You sure know how ta drink ya spirits there, lass. Do you have a name?" His suggestive smile indicated he wished to go upstairs with her like the barmaid did with so many patrons.

Although Aveline's brain was fuzzy, she knew to hold her tongue.

Where was Molly? Aveline refused to wish for Ciarán's presence, although his name fluttered into her mind.

She looked the large man up and down. "No."

"'Tis mighty strange a woman as comely as you wouldna have a name." He lowered his voice. "Aye, you will end up tellin' ya name ta me sometime tonight. Whether it be betwixt the covers, or in the jacks, is anyone's guess."

His words made her blush. His pungent breath caused her to swoon while the alcohol in her system mixed together and caused a bout of nausea.

Aveline put her hands around the decanter to pour another glass, and noticed the container was empty. She saw the man lift a large hand and place it on her thigh but discerned a familiar face grab the man's hand in an iron grip before she could push it away.

Ciarán's voice made the hairs on her neck stand up. "I would not touch her if I were you." Her rescuer—no rescuers—had come through the door without her seeing them, but nonetheless she was glad they arrived.

"Get ya grubby hands off o' the woman, you scum!" Mr. MacRory chimed in.

Ciarán gave the Scotsman a look saying, I can handle it on my own. Mr. MacRory nodded quickly.

"I did not do anything ta her!" The large man pulled away. Apparently, he recognized Ciarán. "'Tis you, O'Devlin?"

Ciarán gave the man a look that would have made anyone less dangerous run away. His eyes were wide and his mouth curved upward. "O'course, O'Rooney, who else would you expect?"

"I am ta s'pose the *sasanach* is yas then?" O'Rooney argued. "She sure doesn't 'ave ya name on her, that's for sure."

Aveline felt the tension rising.

Ciarán bristled. "Well, she owns me farm."

O'Rooney stormed from his chair. "*Bollocks!*"

"'Tis the truth. Take it or leave it."

The large man's face became distorted. "You're trying ta steal more from me. I won't believe ya words."

Ciarán pounded the bar. "We've never stolen a lick from you. You've been threatening our lives an' adding interest to the payments we owe for such petty bets. I've been payin' the dues as quickly as I am able ta, but with the high tax on me land, 'tis become bloody impossible to earn enough to survive."

She looked around and noticed many fuzzy faces watching the unfolding scene. The movement made her queasy, so she closed her eyes and just listened to the argument.

O'Rooney eyed her. "So ya 'ave, but you're taxes are none of me concern. Since you're still behind, I get ta 'ave the *sasanach* ta me self."

Bile rose in Aveline's throat.

"Over me dead body!" Ciarán said and flung off his jacket.

Mr. O'Rooney followed suit. Their vests and shirts were next, as they balled their fists in the ready.

Aveline saw a half-clad Ciarán, and she wished to touch him. A blush colored her face even though she feared what would happen next.

👑 👑 👑

In one quick movement, the pub's patrons encircled the crew as O'Rooney's cronies ambled over to join in the fun. Ciarán gave the first jab, and almost caught the larger man's ear. He feigned left avoiding another right cross directed at his nose. The bar stools, Aveline's glass and decanter, as well as nearby tables were scattered in the fracas.

Within the first five minutes, all three of O'Rooney's allies were either writhing on the ground in pain or completely unconscious.

MacRory knocked them out with three right uppercuts to their heads before they were able to blink twice. "That'll do it." The Scotsman preened while he waited for an opportunity to take on another one.

Ciarán barely slipped past a punch from his opponent's wide fist, as the man's knuckle grazed his right cheek. He failed to block his face, because he glanced at Aveline. Tears streamed down her cheeks. "Demmit!" he growled, but he recovered enough to put a right hook in O'Rooney's eye.

O'Rooney staggered from the punch. He fell and landed on his back on a table, splitting the oak into pieces.

O'Rooney struggled to lift himself with a growl, as Molly stomped down the stairs from the pub's inn behind him. A man followed her descent.

Ciarán heard her voice near the bar. "That is enough fightin', lads!"

No one responded.

O'Rooney lifted himself from the broken table and attempted a jab at Ciarán.

The barmaid roared. "Do I not make me self clear enough ta you blockheads?"

They persisted, despite Molly's raised voice.

The jab missed Ciarán by two inches, and he thrust a knee into the large man's gut.

Before long, O'Rooney brandished a busted nose, split lip, and cracked head, not to mention a prominent shiner. The odds remained two to one, because the man's cronies did not rise off the dirty wooden floor.

To Aveline's relief, Ciarán, with the exception of one small cut on his cheek, and Mr. MacRory, except for bruises on his knuckles, went unscathed. She watched with tears, as everything went helter-skelter around her and she feared for MacRory and Ciarán, watching until her eyelids drooped.

The barmaid yelled at the top of her lungs. "Alright, I want all you out o' me pub or I'm calling the constable. Get goin'!"

Molly's loud tone received all their attention, including the patrons who intently watched the scuffle.

O'Rooney gestured for his cronies, who had barely regained consciousness, to get up off the floor and leave. "This won't be the end o' it, O'Devlin." The group limped through the door and the other patrons followed.

When they left, the pub turned eerily still and quiet.

"Well, that was *craic*," Ciarán said to break the silence, after he caught his breath and turned his attention to Aveline. He was bent over, breathing hard. His hair dripped around his head and sweat covered his exposed skin.

She studied Ciarán, trying not to be attracted to him. The fact he was shirtless didn't make matters any easier.

Mr. MacRory pulled on his shirt and sat on a bar stool. "Aye, it was. How ya feelin' Lady Aveline?"

She tried to stand, but held onto the bar for support. "I daresshay, much better than I wassh earlier."

The Irish whiskey was poison, indeed. She felt tired, sick.

Then she heard the Scotsman's rumbling laughter. "What on Earth did you give ta the lass, Molly? 'Twould be a miracle if she was able ta walk out o' here on her own."

Ciarán glowered in Molly's direction and spoke for a second time since the row. "She gave Aveline *Éireannach uisce beatha.* Irish whiskey."

Molly feigned complete innocence. "You always seem ta ruin me own *craic.*" She winked at Aveline. As Molly cleaned the large mess, her skirts swooshed about the room.

Aveline wondered if the woman ever ceased vying for every man's attention.

But Ciarán didn't have his eyes on the barmaid. His eyes were focused on her.

"Maybe we know you better than you think we do." Mr. MacRory chuckled. "Come on, you two, we best be gettin' back ta the farm an' ta bed."

Aveline knew Ciarán's silence indicated he was not in a very good mood. Who would blame him? Especially when he fought his rival to protect an Englishwoman's honor.

"I am sshure I can manage by mysshelf." She managed to stand and slowly walked out the front door. "Have a good night, Molly, and thankssh for the wonderful drink."

The barmaid stifled a chuckle.

Aveline turned around to say something else and tripped on a rock in the drive.

Ciarán caught her in mid-fall and pulled her upright. He half-supported her as they headed toward the buggy.

The ride home was a bit too silent for her tastes, but Aveline could think of nothing to say that would alleviate the Irishman's anger.

Chapter 16

Aveline bid Mr. MacRory farewell and walked into the farmhouse after Ciarán.

The intensity of Ciarán's anger caused her to tremble. Or maybe she was just cold. Her wrap was much too thin. She should've worn her cloak.

As soon as the farmhouse door closed behind them, he turned to her. *"Tabhair póg dom,"* he whispered. The Gaelic words broke through the silence.

His husky tone flabbergasted her. "Beg your pardon?"

"I told you to kiss me, *cailín*." He pulled her into his arms and crushed his lips to hers in a heated fury. His hands caressed her cheeks.

She ran her hands over his bare shoulders and twirled her fingers in the tufts of hair curling against his neck. The dusty air filled her nostrils with the smell of fresh hay, and she heard the wind whistling against the window pane. Every inch of her body tingled. Then the world around her ceased to exist.

She leaned into his kiss. For the longest time she'd wanted to kiss him again.

She loved when they argued, and she loved when he was angry, because each time he would resolve the situation by kissing her. He placed so much passion into the embraces that she never wanted him to stop.

A growing heat speared through her abdomen. Her body yearned for more.

Somehow, she managed to regain her senses and pushed away from him. "Please. Stop."

At once, Ciarán's hands slid down her arms and came to rest at his sides as he stood looking into her eyes, a smug expression on his face.

What did he see? No doubt her cheeks and lips were reddened as her long hair flowed freely down her back. She felt as wanton as Molly and probably looked it.

"Why did you go to the pub alone, *cailín*?"

His voice seemed like a musical melody to Aveline. "The reason is not important any more, Ciarán."

What was the matter with her? She'd been acting like a barmaid with this man. Gentle bred Englishwomen didn't kiss poor Irish farmers. But maybe if she remained in Ireland, there would be a chance for a future with him. Eventually, the estate in England would become government property. She could change her name to one more suitable for the circumstances, and an Irish clergyman could marry them. Whether it was possible or not, nothing could have prevented her from hoping.

"You knew going alone to the pub at night would be dangerous," he said.

Did she detect concern in his lilting voice? Her eyes roamed downward. Why hadn't he covered himself? His chest was dusted with dark hair. The same arms that had held her moments before were taut with fine muscle. She wanted to caress every inch of his skin.

"Yes, but some thoughts are better left drowned in spirits."

His laughter echoed throughout the living room, alleviating the awkward silence.

Did he mock her? She'd better speak before he inquired further. Her eyes met his.

"You know that universal truth better than anyone."

The stubborn man picked up the shirt he'd dropped on the floor when he kissed her and shrugged into it without buttoning the front.

She smoothed down her skirts, still swaying from the burning sensation he'd left on her lips. "Besides, nothing I do should matter to you in the least. You are certainly not my guardian."

"I may not be ya guardian, *cailín*, but last time I checked you were in me own country an' without a ken as to the people here."

His calm manner mystified her. Had he recovered from his ire solely upon one breathtaking kiss? She'd barely recovered enough of her senses to carry on a conversation.

"My mother was Irish. I know about your people, Ciarán. I am not daft!"

"Right," he sneered. "You must've

186

learned quickly, because I swear you knew nothing about us when you first came here."

She felt vulnerable, and a single tear dripped down her right cheek. "I knew enough! My mama was from this very town. Her name was Carrigan Hughes." Aveline remembered the picture she left in England of the smiling woman with auburn hair.

Ciarán's eyes roamed her face as he lifted his right hand.

She pulled away from the gesture and took a step back.

He remained in place, but his hand dropped. Even if he meant only to wipe the tear away, she couldn't allow another touch to leave her even more defenseless.

Yes, she was half-Irish. His prejudices against the English must've crowded the notion from his mind altogether. To think, she had been contemplating marriage with the man!

She waited patiently for his reply, but

none came. She wanted to retreat to her bed-chamber, curl into a ball, and weep.

Then, he spoke in a soft undertone. "Aveline, promise me we'll not argue any-more." He didn't smile, nor did he frown.

Before she could retort, his words wrapped around her heart like a silk glove. Her eyes closed. "I cannot..." With a sigh, she said. "I promise, Ciarán."

The room went still. By the time she opened her eyes, he'd gone upstairs and left her standing alone. But she wouldn't follow him this time.

Chapter 17

Afton watched Lady Aveline walk toward him in the dim sunlight. A slight mist covered the field. He had expected her tardiness. The previous night's excursions had affected them all. He wondered what happened after he left her with a furious O'Devlin. She was in one piece. A good sign. In all reality, she looked absolutely radiant. Not exactly the look of someone who had received one of the Irishman's dressing downs.

"Good morning to ya, Lady Aveline," he said.

Her hands self-consciously tried to smooth down the many wrinkles in her skirts. "Good morning to you as well, Mr. MacRory."

Afton opened the barn door for her. He bent to gather a pitchfork and sickle from the floor. "You look very bonnie this morning, lass. I ken you slept well last night?" He turned his head to get a better glance. No bruises or cuts were upon her dainty face. Another good sign.

She watched him with raised eyebrows. "Yes, I believe I did."

He nodded as they walked outside and he set down the equipment near the fields of barley. "Aye, 'tis wonderful to hear. None too many who face O'Devlin are able ta walk a night after a row with the man. You saw ya self the very fact in the pub. He looked none too happy with the likes o' you, though. The circumstances dinnae bode well in the end."

He kept his eyes on her as he checked the golden plant's height. Three feet high. The ears drooped and fell doubling back against the straw, meaning the barley was ripe.

She glowered at him. "The man would never hurt a soul. I cannot believe you would say something so utterly untrue about him!"

"Nae, I'm not sayin' it be true. He hadna laid a hand on me afore either, but the blather from the others makes me wonder 'bout his temper." Afton occupied himself with a sickle. He whacked at the first row of brittle stalks. Later, it'd be bound in sheaves with oakum twine and set up in shocks to dry.

Lady Aveline crossed her arms over her chest. "Why does everyone hold him to such high regard if you believe him a vile person?"

He worked as he talked and finished another line. "He puts fear in ta all o' our hearts an' respect in ta all o' our minds. 'Tis why he's such a great leader here. In all actuality, his brothers owe him their lives an' by the rising o' the moon, I wouldna trust me life with any other person who can be found on the Earth."

She placed hands on her hips. "Then why were you so worried something would happen to me in Mr. O'Devlin's presence?"

Afton chuckled. "He still believes you to be a land stealer. He hears ya last name an' thinks o' his dear friend. After all, the Englishman took his family's property from right under his nose. I worry for you, lass." He cut down another row.

She watched him work. "Worry for me? I daresay I can handle my own against Mr. O'Devlin, if that is what you're implying."

Afton was on the next line, but he kept a loose eye on the lady. Luckily, his strength hadn't ebbed. "Physically, lass, the man is unpredictable. Emotionally, you can become lost at sea. He doesna do attachment verra well, if at all."

She picked a loose ear of grain from the ground and twisted the brittle leaves between her fingers. "Oh, I see."

Aveline compared Ciarán to the barley plant. Brittle, but used in many different ways. The poor man knew only heartbreak and loss. No wonder he was so insufferable. She wished there was a way to make him see she'd never hurt him, but an Englishwoman could hardly make any promises to an Irishman that he would believe.

The day continued on as any other. But the clouds that hung high over the moors didn't hold in the rain until nightfall like before. They dipped lower above the field and she felt droplets on her skin.

The workers continued their duties even

though water soaked their clothing.

Aveline hadn't spent much time in the rain when she was in England. Her father had kept her inside to prevent illness. She wanted to run in the grass and feel the rain cascading around her. Instead, she remained working as her dress stuck to her frame.

She glanced at Mr. MacRory. She noticed he always wore green and red tartan trousers with white stockings and black brogues. The pants were faded from long hours in the dirt—rain or shine—and the same for his shirt. Nonetheless, he looked quite picturesque as he stood straight-backed, watching her from a regal height. He set his shovel down and rubbed his beard.

The rain stopped in just a few minutes. Ireland's weather was very strange indeed. Aveline wrung out her drenched hair and skirt. The garments clung to her body like a second skin. She felt exposed and wrapped her arms about herself for modesty.

Squinting past Mr. MacRory's shoulder, she watched Ciarán as he worked in the distance. His hair and clothing were also saturated from the rain. Across the fields, his head turned toward her. He smiled when their eyes met.

👑 👑 👑

After supper, Aveline found Miss O'Grace washing dishes in the kitchen. "What do you know of my mother, Carrigan Hughes? I know she grew up in this village, but nothing else about her."

Miss O'Grace dried her hands on the white apron. "I knew you'd be askin' me soon." She returned the clean cooking ware to its rightful place on the stone wall. "Miss Hughes lived with her father in a cottage across the road. Not more than a few minutes away from this farm. O'Devlin considered her like a mother, you know, ever since she started coming around an' taking care o' him. They remained close until Lord Peyton offered for her hand in marriage." She was honest, at least. "'Twas her father who was the local rector in town an' he taught his daughter to care for others around them more misfortunate."

Miss O'Grace paused. "She was older than Mr. O'Devlin o' course, but the age difference hadn't stopped them from getting on well. She promised always to watch over him, sendin' him food, an' clothing. 'Til she left Ireland forever."

She walked closer, talking as she did. "O'Devlin thought Miss Hughes forgot all about her people. All about him. Then, she bore you an' lived no more. I believe a part o' him blames you for her loss. Well, among the other reasons he doesn't care to admit to any o' us. We all know 'twas not ya fault, lass, but he is too stubborn to let go o' his grudges against you."

Aveline felt the maid's warm arms encompass her. The kind gesture prevented her tears. "Thank you, Miss O'Grace."

"You'll do just fine, dearie." Miss O'Grace released her then turned to complete her chores.

The information Aveline had learned was an explanation for everything she'd been wondering about for the past few weeks regarding Mr. O'Devlin's feelings. The Irishman was determined to find something he did not like about her, as he tried desperately to protect his own heart. At least he found her likeable enough to hold in his arms while they shared a stolen kiss.

Chapter 18

The barley had matured during the past few weeks and was ready for harvesting. Aveline watched Mr. MacRory to learn his technique and was very impatient to get started with the harvest. Ciarán and his brothers usually helped with the harvest, but four people couldn't reap fifteen acres of crops in time for the farmer's market. Not without outside assistance. Neighbors were scarce due to their properties being seized and landowners were not generous with their workers. So Aveline insisted on helping as well.

Taking the bundled sheaves of barley, Mr. MacRory taught her how to stack the straw in shocks. He made an opening from top to bottom—using another bundle in the center for support—and drew the stack upwards, leaving a hollow.

He crouched and pointed at a section. "Leave two holes near the bottom for air circulation. 'Tis a verra good way to prevent overheating an' staleness."

She wiped a hand across her forehead. "What happens when the plant turns stale?"

He stood. "The grain is unfit to sell, becomes animal feed, an' the price drops drastically."

Her lips pursed. "Oh, I see."

The Scotsman created about fifty stacks before quitting for the noontime meal.

Instead of joining them for lunch, Ciarán headed for the barn where he looked after the livestock, working with the dairy and meat. He busied himself with gathering eggs and procuring milk. No doubt to avoid her, Aveline mused. Mr. MacRory washed his face in the water barrel on their way to the farmhouse. Apparently, he'd noticed her watching Ciarán disappear into the barn. "Don't fret, lass, the man knows how everything works on the farm an' doesna allow any o' us to forget the fact." She heard Ciarán's voice in her head. "Remember, *cailín*, me very own family used their bare hands for years cultivating the field you stand on." Every word would have been laced with undertones. Of course, she only imagined the words, but a part of her knew he'd say them if given the chance.

After working with the barley for a sennight, Aveline joined the men on the other crops. They spent a fortnight cutting down oats, wheat, and flax with sickles. Then, they stacked the sheaf bundles. Of course, she was not permitted to do more than hand sheaves over to the four men who piled them. Although she now knew how to stack a shock, her farming naïveté was too much to overlook with time of the essence.

Constant cloud cover didn't block the sun's heat, and soon she wished for rain to work in again. Unfortunately, rain would also dampen the straw and slow their progress.

Her legs ached from the constant bending, her arms were on fire from the many times she lifted straw bundles. No wonder she was given the easier job, she thought, wiping her brow.

Ciarán insisted she have a break after a few hours on the task. She agreed without hesitation, wondering why she allowed him to control her so.

During her break, she took the opportunity to look over what she had written the past few weeks. Working on the novel had been difficult. She'd been retiring early, exhausted, and had found little time to write. And even when she had the time, her muse seemed to have vanished from its place on her shoulder. She'd been struggling with a lack of inspiration for weeks.

After he heard the news of Blythe's condition, Vincent spent multiple days in his estate. He hired an assistant to collect debts and rents from all his townspeople, while he filled ledgers with paid statements. The couple went on picnics by the lake and spent long periods of time conversing near the hearth in high-backed chairs. They discovered, with great happiness, many common interests. The love between them grew.

Leigh, Blythe's brother, searched

the countryside for his missing sister, until he found her marriage announcement in Lancaster's newspaper. His anger escalated when he learned she was wealthy and living carefree on the far side of town.

He made preparations for travel with the utmost haste.

Leigh pounded on the large entrance doors of Stanford Estate.

The butler opened them. "Good evening, sir, who would you be calling upon today?"

Leigh smiled. "Lady Stanford, if you would be so kind as to tell her Lord Compton requests her presence."

The butler bowed. "I will announce your arrival, my lord. Your coat, gloves, and hat please."

Leigh nodded and handed him the garments. "Thank you."

The man hung them on the coat rack then disappeared.

Leigh paced the foyer and found the drawing room not one hundred feet away. He took a seat upon an upholstered chair beside a lavishly carved tea table. He shouldn't pry into their lives, but his rights were on the line.

The liquor decanter taunted him to pour a glass. He thought better of the notion, knowing the lord would not be pleased to see a stranger take his precious stash. On second thought...

"Soon, I will make the lord's acquaintance," Leigh mumbled as the door opened.

His sister looked at him with disdain. "I advise you to leave, sir. You are not welcome on my husband's estate."

Leigh stood. "As you well know, my lady, *your marriage is illegitimate without my consent."*

"It cannot be annulled, if that is what you are trying to say." Too bad his sister defended her husband with common knowledge. Leigh knew they married for convenience. They read the banns and signed the special license less than two months after he found her missing.

He stroked his chin. "Be that as it may, the court will not press a marriage any longer until a living caretaker signs the contract. Since I am very much alive, it seems with my word, everything can be annulled and you will be back at home where you belong, in the attic."

His words shocked Blythe, so much

so she did not know what to say.

Leigh offered a pact. "My dear sister, I will not plead to the courts, if your husband agrees to a duel with me tomorrow at dawn on the fields toward the garden wall." An offer she could not refuse.

She gasped. "Vincent would never..."

He reflected on the fact his little sister was always the favored sibling. Their parents had doted upon her and after they thought him dead in Napoleon's war, left her everything in their will. After he returned very much alive, with their parents dead, the only thing he could do was to keep her as his ward and inherit the lands as her beneficiary. "I am afraid he will have no other choice in the matter. You'll explain to him what will happen if he does not agree. Tell him to meet me tomorrow. If he does not show, then you can be sure I will not hesitate to see you again." He hoped he sounded threatening. Maybe he should've spoken louder.

She nodded then collapsed.

Leigh stood and left his sister crumpled upon the floor.

Vincent found her almost a half-hour later, crying, and she told him everything her brother said. He agreed to the duel, choosing his uncle as a second, and a small sword as his weapon of choice.

Blythe covered her nose with a handkerchief. "You mustn't throw your life away so rashly, Vincent!"

His fingers touched her cheek, wiping a tear away. "Why not? The man came to steal you. I cannot allow anyone to come between us, Blythe."

"I love you, Vincent."

"I love you, too." He took her in his arms and they kissed, separating after a few moments. "Now be a good girl, and wait for my return."

👑 👑 👑

After the harvesting was finished, the threshing and dressing of the barley began. Aveline watched as Ciarán checked each shock to insure the stalks were dry enough for the separation of grain from the husks and straw. She heard him speak with his brothers in Gaelic, gesturing to the field with a nod.

In a cleared area, a canvas tarp was laid. The sheaves were broken open and spread onto an oilcloth laid flush with the ground. Aveline found beating the grain an enjoyable experience and liked using a flail—two pieces of wood tied together with a leather thong. One piece of wood served for the handle, the other for contact with the grain. As she beat the stalks, she took out all her frustration with the Irishman on them.

"This one is for his smile," she murmured between strikes. "And these next three are for each time he kissed me when he was angry." It helped keep her sane.

After separating the kernels from the stalks, the ears were moved to the side, leaving only grain and chaff, or husks, on the canvas. Aveline learned that winnowing was very effective for removing the useless husks. The mixture of chaff and grain was tossed into the air on a windy day. The feather light chaff would blow away while the heavier grain fell back to the canvas.

Mr. MacRory took a few ears in his hands. "Watch this," he said and rubbed them together. In less than a few seconds, he spread his palms. The grain and chaff were apart.

"Wonderful!" Aveline smiled. "I daresay we should've done the whole crop in the same manner. We wasted so much time using the oilcloth method."

"Not so fast, lass." He lifted his eyes up from the basket. "'Twould be a waste o' time to use ya palms. With a flail, we finish a whole shock quicker than our wee hands finish a single sheaf."

Aveline gestured with her index finger. "Yes, but..."

His back went rigid as his gaze moved to her side.

Her eyes went to Ciarán as he strode near. More than likely, he wished them to return to work. "You cannot win, MacRory. Don't even try. The woman knows one fixation. She insists on having the last word." His blue gaze met hers. "Am I wrong, Lady Aveline?"

"I...I was explaining to Mr. MacRory..."

She wished the words would come, but the man's voice affected her.

The Irishman cut in. "You see, that's exactly what I mean." His speech disappeared as though she were falling down a cliff. Her eyes closed and the sensation of his hands caressing her face, his calloused touch massaging the gentle hollows in each cheek filled her head. She imagined his warm lips coming down upon her own.

Mr. MacRory cleared his throat, recalling her attention to the task at hand. "I donna mean to intrude on ya wool gatherin', Lady Aveline, but 'tis the right time to break for a wee bite o' food."

Ciarán chuckled. "Indeed. We wouldn't want ta intrude on such splendid work."

Aveline knew he jested, but her thoughts were cluttered with other ideas.

How embarrassing! No wonder he thought her daft. His hands had remained at his side the whole time. She groaned. If he knew what she was imagining, he'd have enough ammunition for a few more arguments.

Her English nose rose in the air. "I believe splendid works come from those who spend more time *thinking* than speaking."

Their gazes bored into her.

Ciarán's laughter disappeared as his eyes locked on hers. "Right. I'll see you both in the field then." His jaw ticked as he walked away.

Mr. MacRory nodded, a smile on his lips. "Well said, lass."

"Thank you," she said.

They walked toward the barn together, laughing.

👑 👑 👑

Saturday—the day of the farmer's market—arrived. The workers packed everything into burlap sacks, glass jars, and baskets.

Then they loaded the produce into the carts.

The time had come to sell what they'd grown and produced at the market in Londonderry. The trip would take them at least three hours travelling time, though the journey seemed to pass much more slowly than that. When they cleared a hill and Aveline saw the village, nestled in the valley below, she was grateful the long journey was almost over. The town reminded her of London with townhomes and businesses crammed together.

The Altmore Farm produce filled three carts, traveling in a caravan with Ciarán driving the lead cart over a large bridge. Aveline wished she had not been stuck on the same cart with him, but the others had covered their passenger seats with goods, thus leaving his the only one open. Luckily, he was not one for words, preferring to speak to those behind them in Gaelic, while she occupied herself with the scenery.

The small road entered into a round-a-bout where they took a right onto an equally small side street. On the riverside, a large market had been set up and people hustled about selling or buying wares.

The Irishman whistled. "Welcome to the Maiden City, Lady Aveline. She's a handsome one for sure." He rose and stretched his back, admiring the view.

They found their reserved space, parked, and took the draft animals from the carts to a place where they could eat and rest. The men removed wooden boards from the carts, and set them over the open backs to display goods. Covering the makeshift tables with red oilcloths, they placed the baskets and other items neatly on top. Townspeople stopped to inspect the produce, or smell the grain, but few made purchases.

Aveline smiled as often as possible to entice customers into buying. Before she could monitor the inventory, the sun dipped into the West. They would've arrived to the market on Friday and sold for two days, but harvest took longer than expected. The market was open Monday through Saturday, because the Irish didn't wish to travel on Sundays, due to the possibility of bad luck.

She was surprised to think Ciarán believed in such superstitions. In England, everyone stayed at a friend's or neighbor's house for brunch on Sunday. Some even traveled a few miles to get there. Afterwards, they'd attend church until shadows followed them home.

In Londonderry, the small shops closed at sundown. Single growers held collection boxes in the crooks of their arms while packing extra produce surrounded by hay into crates, which would be exported to England or the Americas.

Profits consisted of the little amount left over after taxes on land, hired help, and almost everything else. Margins were slim and

a good market day made the difference between a good year and losing the farm to the
tax collectors.

Nodding farewell to those they had
worked beside all day, the group left for
home, arriving at the farm after dark. After
unpacking and storing goods, Mr. MacRory,
and Ciarán's brothers retired to their cottages
outside the farm.

Ciarán was quiet, thinking about the task
ahead as he walked toward the farmhouse.
Entering, he sat at the dining table, counting
the income from the day's sales and separating the profits. Aveline watched him intently
as he handed her a hefty leather purse.

Opening the drawstring, she peered inside. Ciarán wished he could have given her
more than a few glittering silver and gold
coins. She'd appreciate new dresses and

books. Her money would be gone before next season's harvest. His share would become someone else's income sooner than later.

Years ago, he had grown used to the fact he could no more afford luxuries than he could leave his land for greater opportunities.

Aveline closed the pouch, setting it on the table with a hard knock.

He looked up. "What? Not enough." How many articles of clothing did a woman need to buy anyway? Well, from his experience they wore three at one time, not counting stockings or shoes. Oh, how he wished to see what she looked like under the faded brown dress she wore nearly every day.

She bit her bottom lip. The small gesture made his heart hammer. "No, I..."

"This is a family farm, Aveline. We make enough coin here to survive on." He shrugged. "I've split the profits in an even manner." Why did she hesitate?

Aveline leaned near him, taking a deep breath. "Ciarán, please take my fifty pounds an' pay O'Rooney the last of your debt."

At first, he couldn't believe his ears. She wished to offer all her earnings to him without any conditions? An Englishwoman raised in a rich society who wished to share her wealth? Maybe she was daft after all. He shook his head. "A working man never takes coin from a woman. Why must you damage a man's pride a second time?"

Those beautiful lips puckered. "I don't understand. How has this anything to do with your pride?"

Ciarán smoothed a hand down his face. "First, you insult me in front o' me friend when you blathered about thinking before speaking. Don't think I missed ya hidden meaning, Aveline. I know damn well you believe me ta be a fool." He stood. "Second, you offered me ya wages. A man should be able ta support himself without a woman's help." *Especially not yours.* "What am I ta do with you, *cailín*?"

She smiled. "You know that I don't think you're a fool. I daresay any worker's debts are placed on the owner's shoulders. Theoretically, I'm the one who pays you, and I say you need an additional benefit."

He let out a deep sigh. "Right, well perhaps you speak true."

Aveline obviously knew how to convince a man to change his mind. Maybe it was the way her mouth creased in such a seductive manner, or the way her eyes sparkled in the candle's light. His breeches felt a bit snug, too.

Her gaze met his. "Before my father...left...I wished more than anything to publish a novel, a silly fancy for a woman. Unlike most others, marriage wasn't on the forefront of my mind." She blushed. "I want to help you, Ciarán. Besides, if you had enough to save you can eventually buy land."

Ciarán once thought he'd own Altmore Farm a long time ago, but such was not the case. At one point, he believed he knew everything about Aveline. Why did she choose writing novels over marriage? What made her understand he'd want to own land in the first place? He should've taught her how to farm. Not MacRory. Ciarán should've spent more time with her.

His hands thrummed a steady rhythm on the table to take his mind away from his lascivious thoughts. "Many years later with a good amount o' coin, I might get me self somewhere," he said. "For now, I need not worry over the future when me past is still haunting me, *cailín*."

With a sigh, he held his palm out and closed his eyes. The decision had been made. "Just hand me the satchel an' don't let me see you do so." His hands grabbed the proffered pouch and then he called the maid. He gave Miss O'Grace the bag as she walked over. "You know what to do with this."

"O' course, 'twill be kept for you, Mr. O'Devlin." The maid winked at Aveline and then stifled a giggle. She headed toward the stairs and disappeared from sight.

Ciarán couldn't bring himself to say a word. He took the other pouches lying on the table and decided to hand deliver the money. It was a perfect opportunity to obtain some fresh air. Had he made the right decision? Aveline's funds would pay O'Rooney off for good. No more bar fights, no more threats, no more feeling sorry for himself. The *bastard* could plague someone else with his foul breath and greedy bets.

Ciarán should be pleased with the good luck, but a nagging feeling kept inching into his gut. The night felt different—uncanny— like everything was changing before his eyes. He could no longer ignore his heart.

The farmhouse door opened and closed as a muffled thud echoed in the distance.

Chapter 19

Aveline entered the barn and smelled fresh hay. She collapsed onto a stacked pile, relishing an end to the long day. She still wanted Ciarán to answer all her questions. Why did he avoid her when they worked on the farm? Why did he take the money and walk away? Did he wish she never came to Ireland? Why was he still in the barn?

Her entry apparently hadn't aroused his curiosity. He leaned sideways with an arm propped against a stack of empty wooden barrels. His stance reminded her of the first time they met. Like before, he threw his jacket on a hay bundle, and rolled his shirt halfway up his arms. The fabric was a dusty brown from dirt. He bowed his head for a long while, and she thought him asleep.

She saw a movement in the barn's doorway. A small girl's head peered around the corner, eavesdropping. Her face looked familiar. It was the same child from the boat's lookout months ago. A mass of curly raven hair fluttered behind her.

Aveline blinked. *Who are you?* she asked, but the apparition only giggled then vanished.

Aveline's eyes landed on the Irishman's shocked face. *Why is he so pale? Did he see the same vision?*

Slowly, his head rose and his eyes met hers. He must not have noticed the little girl's presence in the doorway. He probably wouldn't look at Aveline if he had. Maybe he was just surprised she'd followed him.

He walked in her direction, his movements slow, deliberate. "You followed me into the barn, Aveline," he said in a quiet tone of voice, almost as if he had just awakened from a deep sleep. "Why?"

She looked toward the door again. "Why are you here?" She had intended the question for him, but again she noticed the girl's movement. A shiver ran through her as Ciarán approached and she remembered they were under a small child's close scrutiny. She glanced at the doorway again.

He followed her gaze. The beautiful child came into full view, her white dress flowing behind her. Disregarding the stunned look Ciarán gave her, Aveline walked closer to the doorway as the girl ran into the night. She was determined to discover the girl's identity and origin, so she followed.

"Where are you going, Aveline?" Ciarán

asked. His footsteps followed close behind.

As they walked into the quiet night, a soft breeze caressed Aveline, tamping down the heat that had surrounded her a few minutes before.

She stood in the middle of the path leading toward the farmhouse and watched the girl's shape vanish mid-run. The trill of childish laughter echoed in the distance. Even with all the questions running through Aveline's head in the ensuing pervasive silence, there was no doubt in her mind that the running girl was her future daughter.

In fact, Aveline realized, she was *their* future daughter—hers and Ciarán's.

Why would an unmarried woman see her future child? Surely she'd imagined everything. *A wistful mind doesn't make one mad, does it?* A sick feeling settled in her gut.

Aveline turned toward Ciarán. Understanding showed in his smile. "I need to know who the girl in the doorway is."

His eyes looked reflective. The moonlight danced within their blue depths. "I've only seen her once before meself."

Aveline smiled. "You mean to say you've seen a little girl in a white dress before?" She felt a chill even though the breeze had dissipated with the child.

He sighed. "Yes."

In all her days, she hadn't known a man who'd admit such a thing. From her minimal experience anything involving children didn't appeal to young men, except those conversations involving the mention of heirs.

"May I ask when, Ciarán?"

His loose hair shook as he nodded. "During our picnic. Ya bonnet became an apparition. I saw you run after a little girl with black hair an'..."

Aveline finished his sentence. "...blue eyes."

He burst into laughter. "Good to know I didn't get as foxed as I first thought."

She wanted to smack him for such a comment. "I'll have you know you're an insufferable Irishman!"

A shadow crossed his features. "I know I've been unpleasant these past couple o' months." He paused. "Will you forgive me?" His voice sounded strained.

She should, she thought, probe the matter further, but she yearned to comfort him instead. At least he was willing to acknowledge his misgivings. "Yes, I will."

Not a single muscle in his lean frame twitched for a moment. Then, he held out his arm. "Let us return to the barn, Aveline."

She clung to him. "Is she real?"

"I can't say," he said.

Entering the barn, they walked back to the same hay pile. She bent and picked up a perfect red rose, sharing a stem with two closed buds, lying on the hay.

She avoided the thorns and took a deep whiff of the fragrant smell.

A sigh passed her lips as Ciarán took the bloom and inspected it. He muttered under his breath as he kissed the rose and placed it in a wall crack.

Aveline didn't add superstition to her growing list of inquiries. Her need to touch Ciarán overcame all rational thought.

Chapter 20

Aveline hesitated, but Ciarán didn't give her enough time to think, and—like in her daydream earlier—his lips met hers. She felt his work-worn hands grazing her cheeks. His touch left her weak. No matter how much her knees wobbled or her heart fluttered, she couldn't resist kissing him back. For once, his anger hadn't ignited the situation. Grabbing his shirt collars, she pulled him closer.

He fell on his knees, pulling her close.

She savored his body's warmth and the hay's fresh smell mingling with their individual scents of lavender and soap.

He sighed, breaking off the embrace. "Right, well, we've both had a trying day. Without ya help, 'tis hard to believe we would have better results. For that, Aveline, I thank you." He took a shallow breath. "'Twould seem to me a good night's rest is in order for a tired body or...two."

His lips returned to her face and then trailed downward, leaving goose bumps in their wake. Her body molded to his like fine clay. His sturdy frame held her upright when she would've collapsed backward. She needed more from him, but didn't know how to initiate it. "I daresay sleep would receive me with open arms."

He twirled his right hand into her upswept hair and played with it as he deepened the kiss. His left hand explored elsewhere and ended in a rather pleasurable part of her anatomy. Somehow, Aveline noticed his hand roaming toward her abdomen, and a moan escaped her lips.

Ciarán's melodic voice rung in her ear as he trailed kisses down her neck. *"Ba mhaith liom luí leat."*

She moaned again.

"I may not understand the words, but I agree to them wholeheartedly," she murmured as she felt his lips near her bodice.

He chuckled. "The words don't matter, *cailín*. I will show you what the phrase means soon enough."

👑 👑 👑

Ciarán stood and unbuttoned his shirt. He tossed the soiled garment aside and watched her reaction.

Moonlight shone through the partly opened doorway and danced over Aveline's alabaster skin as she sat on the hay, watching him. The blush spreading through her cheeks gave her a childlike appearance. Surely she knew what she did to him. They locked eyes for a moment before he seduced her into another searing kiss.

Her hands moved over his bare chest and wound around his neck. A groan escaped his lips. She leaned into him and he deepened the kiss. She tasted like the finest whiskey, sweet but without the smoky flavor. His tongue slid between her parted lips with ease. She gasped at his intrusion then matched his rhythm with her tongue.

Ciarán took the pins from her hair and the fire flew freely about them. He ran his hands through the mass of curls, relishing its softness. He'd dreamed of this moment every time his eyes closed. Her hair was even softer than he imagined, gliding through his fingers like silk.

"Such beauty could never be surpassed." His body lowered to the hay. Her lithe form followed him down.

The time for him to free her was now or never. Never. With a deft movement, his fingers worked her gown's buttons. He remembered the first day they met. Like a dream, his hand grazed the smooth skin hiding underneath the old brown work gown as the garment slid off her shoulders.

He watched as she pulled away from the kiss and stood. Her cheeks blossomed in color, her rosy lips swollen from his kiss. An impish grin played across her features as her hair fell across her face.

Ciarán thought Aveline would run away, like the innocent maid she was. *Christ, what if she did?* His heart would never forgive him.

Instead her dress and corset were thrown to the floor until only a shift covered her in a translucent sheen. The sight drove him mad with need. He reached out a hand to touch her through the thin material. She thwarted his movement and shed the garment.

The shift fell like a gossamer veil, leaving the slender curves of her body exposed. Her beautiful ivory skin glowed in the moonlight.

"An' neither can a single heart be rendered so helpless from the sight."

She placed the undergarment on the hay beneath them. "Do you write poetry? I daresay any man with such a sweet tongue writes a verse or two every so often."

He winked, keeping his eyes on her face. "'Tisn't something I boast about to the lads."

The dark hair on his torso led to a hidden path under his trousers. Aveline longed to view what he hid from the world. His strong arms lowered her backward onto the hay. Their bodies tangled as he leaned over, kissing every inch of her flesh.

They ignored the chill of the barn as they explored each other. The hay under their bodies provided a fine mattress.

She kept her hands busy while he left a

warm, moist trail down her chest, wetting her breasts. His mouth on her sensitive flesh made her toes tingle. Apprehension hadn't affected her until now. What if she did something wrong?

She ran her hands over his shoulders, wrapping her arms around to touch his back. A burgeoning desire overwhelmed her core. The throbbing sensation made her writhe with eagerness. He continued to nibble a protruding nipple, flicking his tongue back and forth, while using his forefinger to caress the other. The fingers on his other hand ran along her torso until they stopped on the inside of her thigh.

How did one handle such an ocean of feelings?

He hesitated.

"Continue, Ciarán, please." Her heart raced.

He grinned and kissed her, his hand moving between her legs. As he caressed her *down there*, she felt a small part of her soul join with his. She loved his touch. Especially the sensations it stirred within her, as he rubbed his thumb along her tiny nub. His fingers stroked and caressed until passion gripped her in rippling waves.

His body rocked against her the more her hands met his skin, and she felt as if she were an irresistible woman, the kind a man loves and cherishes forever.

Suddenly, he removed his fingers and pulled away. No! Why would he stop so soon?

"Aveline, you don't know what you do to me. There is so much more you must learn before..."

She felt empty without his caress, her shuddering body writhing for more. "Please, teach me."

Apparently unable to resist her, he removed his trousers, exposing his manhood that protruded from a dark patch of hair between his thighs. Shifting his body, he parted her legs with his knees then bowed his head and kissed her full on the lips. His tongue caressed her mouth as a mounting pressure grew from within her. When she moaned, he entered her with a quick thrust. The sharp pain made her wince. *What did he do?* She stiffened, resting her head against his chest. Aveline could hear his ragged breaths against her ear.

He hesitated, using the pad of his thumb to stroke her cheek. The gentle touch lessened her apprehension enough for her to allow him to continue. She followed his slow movements with her hips and the tingling ache subsided into a whole new wave of pleasure.

Their hearts beat in tandem as each slow thrust increased the friction, heat, and desire until she was mad with need.

She imagined they were alone on a soft pillow of clouds, protected against the outside world. There were no cares or bothersome worries about how to survive. There was only the two of them and this all-encompassing hunger for each other.

She shuddered and her body exploded into pinpoints of light as Ciarán gave way to his release in her arms. As her trembles started to subside, he moved just so against her and a shattering wave of pleasure, more intense than before, crashed through her system, sending her back into orbit. She wished to go on feeling this way forever.

👑 👑 👑

Ciarán watched a smile grace her lips. Her eyes were closed. Each delicate freckle enhanced her overall angelic image. Her hair outlined her head with copper waves. Womanhood suited his Aveline.

He heard her breathing slow and knew she slept. Her scent remained on his skin. He would be reluctant to wash it off.

Slipping from her embrace, he donned his trousers before he turned toward her slumbering form. He gathered her garments, covered her nakedness, and lifted her into his arms, though he regretted disturbing her peace.

"C'mere, *cailín*, 'tis best we don't sleep where others will find us in the mornin'," he whispered as he walked toward the farmhouse, knowing she'd wake beside him the next day.

Ciarán wanted her to remember every loving detail. More importantly, he wanted her to beg for more.

He climbed the staircase sideways, so her limbs wouldn't hit the walls, and deposited her slowly and gently upon the bed in his chamber. He removed his clothes and crawled under the quilt beside her, his arms wrapped around her waist. She snuggled against him, and his lust returned. He recalled the way his body writhed with such a lovely woman in his arms. The thoughts would plague him all the rest of the night, as well as for many nights to come.

Knowing he couldn't take an exhausted woman as she slept, he thought on other more pressing matters—something guaranteed to drench his ardors in cold water. What to do about the marriage question?

He knew a night such as they just shared could never come to pass again unless the banns were read. Her ladylike upbringing wouldn't abide otherwise. Blast! Not to mention, Lord Peyton would look down upon him with aversion. The man had been like a father to him. And of course he'd insist on marriage.

Ciarán didn't have the luck of the Irish when women were involved in his life. He was too emotional for a man—too demmed caring or not caring enough, he wasn't sure which—especially when she considered him so insufferable.

He vowed to find a way for them to be together, but he needed time.

He watched his phantom queen sleep. Her mane was strewn about his pillows like fire. He would never glimpse such splendor again unless a miracle befell him.

But miracles were hard to come by in Ireland.

Chapter 21

Aveline awoke in a very compromising position. Her body was entwined with none other than...Ciarán O'Devlin. Crawling from the bed, she remembered all the details from the night before, except how she ended up lying in the upstairs bedchamber.

She needed to face him about the incident. She could not keep on dallying with this man when he was not her husband. Could she run the farm knowing what happened between them? Knowing he didn't feel the same?

She watched him sleep a couple minutes longer. Was she in his dreams?

Standing, she noticed there was blood on her thighs. Her *virginal* blood. "Oh no!" She gasped as the enormity of her actions hit her, and she quickly found a robe to pull about her.

Ciarán awoke to her exclamation. "Why are you awake, luv?" His voice was husky, as he crawled from bed. The way he pronounced "love," made her heart melt for him again.

He stood nude, shameless.

She raked her eyes over his body. She had once thought the moonlight accentuated his features, but now she noticed that the sunlight streaming through the opened window highlighted every corded muscle. The hair on his body glowed so black it looked dark blue. His eyes had become a light gray.

She imagined him touching her again. In her mind's eye, he pulled her hair back from her face, kissing her lips until they reddened. She could feel him inside her as his raw heat spread waves of pleasure up and down her body. Maybe they could spend the day in bed, discovering each other...again.

Ciarán smirked and she collapsed back into reality. "There are chores to do before next season's crops are planted, and I...ah...need to start on them as soon as possible. The barley grew so...wonderfully, I would not like to ruin the next crop by not preparing the land in time."

Ciarán advanced. "Nonsense! You are the farm's owner..."

Aveline could not believe she heard him mention her status with a straight face.

"...an' you should not be working in the fields. You most certainly do not have to worry over such matters. Tell MacRory to start on the chores today an' spend the time with me." Did he want her to lay with him the rest of the day? Did he choose not to work instead?

Maybe he cares for me after all. No, such a simple trick would not catch her unawares. She was a weak woman indeed. "I would never ignore the chores or my duty to this farm!"

He must know she would not choose to stay abed with him when the farm that provided their food and shelter needed attention.

He sighed, as he grabbed a shirt and trousers from the pile beside the bed. "Suit ya self, *cailín dathúil.*"

She stopped him before he placed his arms through the shirt sleeves. "I do believe we have an important matter to discuss, Ciarán," she said and gestured toward the bed.

His confused look indicated he didn't perceive their coupling as significant. He cocked an eyebrow, daring her to protest.

"You do not have any regrets about last night, do you?"

Surely, he had noticed her innocence and took advantage. An untried woman who is now ruined and unable to marry. But she didn't say it. Her pride prevented such an admission. Besides, she would've repeated the wonderful act if given the chance and she knew it. "Of course not, why should I?"

👑 👑 👑

Ciarán wished to undress her and pull her toward the bed. He knew now what she hid underneath her work day clothes. A simple sliding motion of her garments would show him everything. But any visceral thoughts were doused when Aveline spoke.

"We are to be married secretly, after all. Am I right?" Innocence shone in her eyes. Her wistful attitude unsettled him. Her simple solution would hardly work even in his own culture. She wouldn't seriously entertain such a whimsical idea, would she?

But he knew his response wasn't what she wished to hear, so he remained silent.

She smiled and laughter danced in her eyes. "Do you not agree I could change my name and remain in Ireland with you?"

The woman read too many romantic novels and wrote about too many perfect relationships, he thought. Didn't she understand there could be no happy endings with him?

She had refused a day in bed together, but it was all he could offer.

Her mouth trembled when he didn't respond. Ciarán was a hardened man and not a single tear could sway him. They were a woman's way of receiving immediate reconciliation. What could he say to assure her of his intentions?

"I think you take things a bit too far, *cailín*."

She crossed her arms. "No. I do not. You

did that on the day you first kissed me."

The words stung him.

"A kiss does not mean anything! You enjoyed those kisses as much as I did. 'Tis a way to pass the time."

She bit her lip. "Yes, I daresay I enjoyed it too much, then." He heard the hiccup in her voice.

Ciarán bowed his head. "You don't want someone like me in ya life, Aveline."

"Do you love me?" she asked.

The question lingered too long without an answer as Ciarán winced. Love an Englishwoman and contradict everything he stood for? Before meeting Aveline the thought had never crossed his mind, but recently everything had changed.

The real question was, did Aveline love him?

Last night, when he vowed to find any way possible for them to have a future, he'd meant it. But he was unable to give her any hope, because he couldn't see a way for them to be together. He wouldn't lie to her, so he said nothing.

She owned the very farm he put his whole life into. What if he said the wrong thing and she forced him into the street? Would that be the worst she could do to him? He almost laughed, thinking she could put him out on his arse.

Then he imagined her grabbing hold of his ear and pulling him through the door like the headmistress in the Catholic boarding school he had attended as a boy. Quite frankly, the thought made him tremble, and the words came before he could think. "I cannot say I love you, because if I did, there is nothing we could do about it."

He knew hurting her would hurt him worse, but he was already knee deep in the mud. Ciarán had sworn never to gamble with his heart. But sacrifices for the greater good were part of life. *His* life.

Aveline's face reflected his words' effect. "So, you do not love me, and you do not want to marry me?"

Her words felt like a blow to the ribs. *Not true*, he wanted to say, but his breath caught in his lungs and he could not speak.

She sighed. "Oh, bother, why do I even try for propriety? My father would've been very disappointed in us, Ciarán. I did hope everything would turn out better. You are a far superior manager than I could ever become. Tell the lads I am giving the farm to you, because after today I can no longer reside here."

Aveline cannot give away land through a verbal contract. The demmed government banks need a written signature.

His accent became heavier with emotion. "What is all this blather about me owning the farm? It's in ya father's will, Aveline. You have this farm for life, an' I refuse to go against his word." He stepped closer. "You cannot just pack ya bag an' leave."

If she left, how would he survive without her?

She flinched. "Why ever can I not? My purpose here is done. The English do not belong on this soil, because all we do is quarrel with one another. We cannot seem to live in harmony, even though my papa thought otherwise."

His whole world crumbled around him. "I don't understand how."

She glared at him without sympathy. "Nor shall you ever understand me, Ciarán." She walked to the door still wearing his robe.

He watched her step through it. Every instinct he had pushed him to stop her from leaving, but his pride held him back.

"Oh, and one more thing." Broken and on the edge of tears, her angelic face peered through the opening. "In case your brain is too filled with other thoughts, since I remain unmarried and am now evidently ruined, I am now destined to live on the streets. After all, my father did say I was to inherit his estate and lands *only* upon my wedding day." Without another word, she quit the room.

He didn't believe her. It couldn't be true. Her father would never be so cruel. *She deserves much better than me anyway. In time, she will forget I ever existed.*

A small voice in the back of Ciarán's mind protested that he loved her. Maybe he should go to her and try to talk this out. But no, he was too late. Miss O'Grace would be awake and too much suspicion brewed about their relations already for him to chance the woman seeing him alone with Aveline.

He'd never hear an end to the maid's words. Aveline would never listen to what he said. He'd managed to turn her completely against him.

Picking up her shift, he saw the telltale sign of her lost innocence and threw the garment against the wall.

He exploded with anger. "*Bagtard*! The colleen is mad to return home without means." Thinking better of the action, he retrieved the shift to add to the burn pile. He scratched his mussed hair and dressed, trying to change his fate enough to prevent her departure.

Chapter 22

Aveline hurried to her room and locked the door. Parchment covered her writing table, each sheet a part of her almost finished novel.

The ending now shone clearly in her head. She must finish the story before leaving the farmhouse. Not that it was likely Ciarán would chase after her. The Irishman had made his feelings as clear as a summer sky in June.

With quill in hand, she quickly scribbled it down.

At dawn the next day, Blythe quietly followed behind her husband as he walked to the clearing where Leigh waited. Scents from the nearby flower garden accosted them as Vincent approached her brother.

Earlier, Vincent had embraced her and told her his farewell. She knew she could not slumber while her husband risked his life to keep her safe.

As the two men met, she hid behind a tree and heard every word.

Leigh walked closer. "So, I finally make my acquaintance with the elusive Lancaster."

"Yes, it's been too long. I've heard much about you." Vincent's self-assurance shone in his rigid stance. She loved his sturdy exterior.

Leigh smirked. "No doubt my sister likes to talk."

"I do not wish to fight you, Compton, but you give me no other choice. I must protect them *at all costs." Vincent lunged with his sword toward Leigh's heart, but he feinted right, as he thrust the sword into midair.*

Blythe gasped into her palm.

Leigh aimed his sword toward Vincent's neck blocking with his stroke.

The struggle continued until Leigh spun around, missing a hit directed toward the face, meanwhile jabbing the sharp point into Vincent's abdomen. Taken aback by the collision's force, the older man fell onto the ground. With his sword raised high into the air, Leigh attempted a killing blow.

Blythe couldn't sit and watch the

life seep from her husband. After all, he didn't truly expect her not to follow him.

She knocked her brother to the ground. She didn't care whether she harmed him or not. Kneeling with Vincent's head in her hands, she smoothed the slick hair from his brow. Sweat covered his face as he looked at her with the blue eyes she'd always loved. But their luster was gone.

He faded while Leigh struggled to stand and finish the job.

"I love you, Blythe," Vincent said as his eyes closed tight.

Her brother pointed his blood-tipped sword in Vincent's direction. "Well, isn't that just romantic? A real tragedy if you ask me. Nothing in this world goes according to plan, does it, Blythe?"

She rested her husband's head on

the ground. "No, it certainly does not." She picked up Vincent's sword and pierced her brother's heart. With a cry, his body went still. She'd ended his life to save the man she loved. Very romantic, indeed, and rather foolish, too.

In the past, she avoided love like bad spirits. When she met Vincent, everything changed.

In the coming days, she nursed him back to health. She spent her days wiping his brow and feeding him soup. Soon, the fever subsided and his wound healed. He had depended on her strong-will and he lived as a result.

Their son, Alasdair Stanford, was born the following year.

She learned almost too late that she was the writer of her own destiny. An existence that started off none too happy, but in the end became all the more worthwhile.

Aveline set down her quill. *I am the writer of my own destiny, too,* she mused. She stacked the paper in numerical order and placed a ribbon around the bundle with a small note, crying for the novel she would leave behind. Ciarán needed to know her true feelings from the inside out. Then she dressed and packed a satchel. *But my destiny is one where love is unrequited and lost.*

A knock sounded on her door. All her hopes centered on Ciarán being there when she answered. "Yes. Who is it?"

"Miss O'Grace." You aren't at breakfast, is anything the matter?" The Irishwoman never let anyone miss a meal.

Aveline opened the lock, let the maid in,

and closed the door behind her. "May I ask you a question?"

No doubt the woman's eyes had found her satchel lying on the bed, but she only nodded.

"Did you find my mother very agreeable, Miss O'Grace?" Aveline knew she must've looked bedraggled, but she kept the robe about her shoulders. Surely the servant noticed it was not her own.

Miss O' Grace sighed. "Yes, I did. Carrigan Hughes was such a fine woman. She was such a looker. Lads about town couldn't keep their eyes off o' her."

Aveline raised her eyebrows. "How did she come to know my father?"

Miss O'Grace smiled. "Oh, five year old Mr. O'Devlin asked her ta eat supper with them on Lord Peyton's first visit. Ya father had owned the land for not half a year when they met. I saw the way he looked her way.

'Twas no doubt he loved her from that moment on."

Aveline would miss the maid's kindness and her crinkling eyes, not to mention her trust.

"Sounds romantic," she said. "Thank you for everything."

The woman looked forlorn. "No worries, Lady Aveline. I'll be seeing you, again." She curtsied and walked toward the door.

Aveline's eyes welled. Her heart would never forgive her for leaving, but she had no choice. "You understand, I must return to England. Really, there is no other way."

Miss O'Grace turned and placed a hand on her trembling one. An embrace would not heal her wounds a second time. "I'll not be stopping you, dearie. You are the only person who knows what ya heart desires."

Chapter 23

Aveline's absence affected Ciarán. With each breath he took, with every beat of his heart, he knew he lived for her alone.

The realization that he'd fallen in love with her hit him harder than ever when MacRory approached him in the grass field.

"Where be Lady Aveline this morning? I dinnae ken why she was to be late onto the fields today."

The Scotsman's pinched eyebrows and

downturned eyes meant more than words.

Ciarán wondered why she hadn't chosen the burlier man. MacRory would've gladly lain with her in the hay. She wouldn't have run away from him, because he wouldn't conceal his love behind a guarded facade.

Blast! He would've killed the Scotsman if he so much as looked in Aveline's direction. No wonder MacRory hadn't wooed her.

Her late parents had left an empty hole in her heart and she needed someone to fill it. But Ciarán hid everything and lost her. He remembered another time when someone had left him behind.

Twenty-three years ago, Miss Carrigan Hughes had been visiting the farm every day to care for them. The last day she came, he'd jumped from behind a hay stack, scaring her in the dark barn. Being nearly eighteen years old, Aveline's mother took his pranks with a smile.

She told him about her upcoming marriage to Lord Peyton, and Ciarán had never forgotten what she said.

"For the moment, I can give you me solemn vow ta always protect you. I love you very much."

Returning to reality, Ciarán shrugged. "She left." He kept his face blank, avoiding emotion like he dodged a hit in boxing.

MacRory rubbed the red hair at his jaw, a gesture he did every time he saw or thought about Aveline. "I donna believe she would fail ta bid me a fine farewell. After all, the lass an' I shared a good amount o' time in each other's presence these last few months. 'Tis a wee bit odd for her to run away, if you ask me." The Scotsman would blame him for her departure if he knew what had happened. "Did she say anything ta you before she went outta sight?"

Ciarán mouthed the word "yes" and MacRory spoke for him. "*Och*, o' course she did. She favored you above the rest o' us.

Did she give you a reason for leavin'?"

Until this point, he'd never felt ashamed around his friend. He rubbed a self-conscious hand through his tousled hair then stood with his arms crossed and his head bowed. "Right, well 'tis true she is gone because o' me." He didn't look the Scotsman in the face. Instead, he looked toward the River Blackwater.

He remembered the day spent there with Aveline. They shared a picnic together on the river bank.

Everyone on the farm had noticed their connection. Not even the daft, dumb, and blind could miss the sparks.

Aveline was stubborn all right. But so was he.

He nearly forgot MacRory's chuckling presence. "You donna say, man. You've got what you'd hoped for all along. Well done lad, you are now in charge o' the farm again."

Ciarán groaned. A bit of delight for

someone's good fortune shouldn't hurt his soul.

MacRory grinned. "You wanted the farm back ever since the bonnie lass arrived."

The statement loomed between them. Before her arrival, Ciarán would've foregone any chance at happiness to work his precious land. What had happened?

He adjusted his flat cap. "My feelings on the matter were different when I first met her. Time passed an'...um...I changed me mind."

His friend chuckled. "Stop beatin' ya self up over everythin', O'Devlin. She'll come back when she realizes she has nowhere else to go. You wait an' see. She'll be knockin' upon the farmhouse doors before you can finish milkin' the cows."

Ciarán laughed without mirth. The words were about as true as a land without rent. Aveline would never return. He might as well be whistling jigs to a milestone.

Chapter 24

Aveline thought running away was a grave mistake, but staying would've been much worse. She felt like the Irish mist upon the moors—her head flowed with uncertainty and confusion rushed over her like gooseflesh as she arrived in Carrickmore. Tired from the walk, she sauntered into town and waited on the cobblestones for a stagecoach. A woman should not be alone in such a place, she decided, wrapping her shawl closer. Unable to mask the negative feelings, she set them free.

One major thought came to mind. Ciarán had never chased after her. The notion pained more than his rejection. He'd followed after her when she ran the first day they met, but the moment she threatened to leave the country, he held his ground. Her heart ached for him, but she had made up her mind. Although, she wished for a different outcome, they obviously had no future.

A shadow covered her as a four-wheeled, black coach stopped. Finally, her conveyance had arrived.

A door opened, steps were lowered, and dread filled her gut as a cloaked man grabbed her. Before she could resist, something connected with her head. Everything faded to darkness.

Aveline awoke in a daze. She was blindfolded and lying on the seat of the moving vehicle, without a notion to how long she had been unconscious. The knot on her head throbbed, but she could not tell if there was blood on her temple because her limbs were tied. Her skin was becoming painful where the cloth cinched around her wrists and ankles. A gag prevented her from yelling for help.

She felt hot breath on her cheek. It smelled like rotten onions. A voice warned her not to move.

She squirmed in the seat. Why had she left the man she'd given her heart to? He didn't want a future, but perhaps she could've persuaded him otherwise.

Father, I wish you were here.

Her father's image came to her mind and she knew the most important answers to her questions were through her memories of him.

Four years ago, during a bout of writer's block, she had been eavesdropping on a commotion downstairs. Her governess, Miss McCork, lead a group of thieves who were stealing her family's heirlooms. A henchman noticed her and threw her in a closet. Fortunately, her father had taken control of the situation and saved her.

If only my father were here to save me now, she thought.

"Whoa boy!" A man who sounded like Eònan stopped the coach. The sudden movement jolted all the passengers forward. His booted footsteps stopped to her right. "What be this nonsense in the road, lad?" he asked someone else through the side window.

So, at least two men were in the carriage with her. She could not guess the cause of their concern, but she knew any distraction they encountered was in her favor.

"There be a person with a cow, sir."

Aveline recognized the younger voice beside her, but before she could put a name to him, Eònan spoke again. "Looks ta be the likes o' a woman. Wonder what she is doin' all the way out 'ere so early? I canna for the life o' me tell who she is wi' that bloody cloak coverin' all o' her head."

Oh no! She couldn't be left alone with the older man.

His footsteps shook the carriage as someone departed. "I will go an' check on the lass blockin' our way," said an older voice. "You make sure the colleen in the back 'ere doesna move a tiny hair o' anythin' before I get back."

"Ya word is me command, O'Rooney." She felt the two younger men's eyes upon her as the one in charge left the coach, leaving an eerie silence.

O'Rooney had kidnapped her!

A muffled thud came from outside the wagon, and someone with shuffling feet opened the door. A curvy body came to sit next to her. A woman's voice said something in Gaelic to Eónan, gesturing to the carriage's compartment. He carried a large bundle past the window and another thud shook the carriage.

Warm hands removed the bindings that held Aveline. With her mouth freed, she whispered the name, "Molly McGuinness" into the dark.

The woman smiled, her voice revealed such effects. "Yes, 'tis me an' none other than Solás and Eonán O'Devlin themselves."

For once, Aveline was glad to see her. "How ever did you know where to find me?" She rubbed her head, noticing the red welts around her wrists.

"O'Rooney has been makin' his plans for a while now," Solás said.

Miss McGuinness nodded. "He be tellin' all o' the people I...spend time with at the pub...about the kidnap, you see. So, I told the only men who were able ta help me. O'Rooney was on his way ta the farm ta get you, when all o' a sudden you appeared before his very eyes on the roadside."

Aveline shuddered. "I am sure the coincidence was quite a convenience for him. I daresay he wanted to kidnap me for a reason."

"Yes," Molly looked at Solás for support. He nodded.

The woman hid her amusement. "Séan O'Rooney, wants his revenge for the last time O'Devlin beat him. Now, he is greedy for more coin. Kidnapping you would 'ave spurred O'Devlin's passions enough ta fight him again. This time, he was ready. As a reward, O'Rooney would receive you."

"What would you have me do then?" Aveline asked.

Miss McGuinness gave her a pointed look. "O'Rooney is not alone, you know, but that fact does not concern me the most 'bout everythin'. Seems 'twould be best for you to leave the country an' return home to England." Then she frowned. "The O'Rooney man is after you for somethin' an' I do not like you disrupting me town because o' it."

She hated to leave her precious farm behind. Most importantly, she did not want to leave her Irishman behind. "You've forgotten I own Altmore Farm..."

Miss McGuinness smirked. "You left the farm for Mr. O'Devlin ta manage, you did."

She wondered what else the barmaid knew. "I haven't any coin, you see. How am I to live?"

"Take this." The woman handed her a leather pouch. "'Tis enough to pay for room an' board until you find employment."

Damn. The woman knows everything about me! Aveline stared at Molly long and hard, before she took the purse and placed it in her satchel. "All right, I'll go. You can have your precious peace back," she said and turned away as her eyes welled.

They drove the carriage north toward the

coast and a waiting ship. Before leaving the carriage, Aveline said, "Please don't tell Mr. O'Devlin my involvement in this matter. It is not my wish to worry him."

❦ ❦ ❦

Solás watched the Englishwoman walk toward the crowded dock.

"Are you sure we made the right decision?" he asked in Gaelic.

Molly also watched the girl. "Yes, we did," she spoke in the same language, tapping the roof with the back of her hand. "All the better for your brother without her. At least, we saved her from that foul man, O'Rooney." She pointed to the tied bundle in the carriage's compartment. "Besides, O'Devlin'll go after her."

He laughed. "You sound regretful, Miss McGuinness."

"I do not make regrets," she snapped. "I

make memories. There is a difference, you know."

Solás nodded. "Right, there is. What if my brother learns his lesson the hard way?"

Molly shook her head. "Men never learn their lessons. Why do you think they so easily gamble their earnings away? A man will never accept defeat until he knows he'll never win."

Chapter 25

Ciarán felt as if he'd live alone forever. Miss Hughes could not protect him from losing the people he cared about most. Yet, perhaps she had protected him, after all, he reflected. Maybe he was supposed to fall in love and marry Aveline. Lord Peyton gave her the farm in his will. Her father had known she'd meet him in Ireland.

If he married her, he'd own the farm. What a fool! Suddenly, he saw the truth of everything Lord Peyton had done for him. Everything Miss Hughes had done for him.

Aveline resembled her mother so much both physically and mentally, but he never blamed her for Miss Hughes's death. He knew how the lack of parents could affect someone. Her kindness had grown on him and he'd taken her for granted. *Damn*!

He performed his daily chores, but thoughts of Aveline clouded his mind with so many memories and impressions that he dropped the water buckets halfway from the well to the stables. Why must she torment him so?

One kiss had brought his temper down. One look had made him feel everything he missed in his life. Yes, he missed his family and friends. Why did his brothers insist on living three miles away in dusty cottages? He'd ample space in the farmhouse for everyone. *And damn again*!

He couldn't keep track of his own brothers. How could he find a runaway English-woman? He needed a pint, or two or three, but the hour waxed late and work started early.

Ciarán looked forward to seeing the fire-haired beauty in his dreams.

👑 👑 👑

County Cumbria, England, 1824:

A large packet ship took her away from Ireland and a stage coach brought her to Peyton Manor. Even though she knew her fate well, she'd never forget the place where her heart resided. She'd never forget the Irishman she had left behind.

The estate loomed before her. Its red-bricked exterior was just as large and welcoming as she remembered. The overgrown lawn glistened in the morning sun, surrounding the cobbled path upon which she walked.

Reaching the front steps, Aveline tried opening the manor's door, but it was locked. "Godfrey, it is Aveline Peyton, please let me in." Her satchel sat on the porch, slumped over in an odd manner reflecting her mood. The journey home had left her fatigued, but she needed to reacquaint herself with the remaining servants.

The butler opened the door a crack. "My lady, is that you?"

She pasted on a smile to hide her melancholy. "Yes, of course. I've returned from overseas."

He opened the door wider, a welcoming smile on his face. "It is such a relief to see you again, my lady."

She walked into the manor house, relishing the childhood home she left behind. "I nearly thought you would've run away like the others."

Godfrey smiled warmly. "Never. Who was to keep the manse while you were gone, then? Surely, Miss Abernathy would not be inclined to clean without proper guidance."

Aveline giggled. "You are right, Godfrey. So Miss Abernathy is still in residence?"

His eyes crinkled. "Yes, she insisted you would return with a handsome fellow on your arm. She's been awaiting your arrival. You see, my lady, we have nowhere else to go." He extended his arms in invitation. "May I assist you with your luggage?"

Godfrey's kind smile resembled Miss O'Grace's.

"Please do. I fear a nap will be upon me within half an hour." She walked up the same flight of stairs she'd known for years. Her bedchamber was on the second floor.

Godfrey lifted her satchel and closed the door. He followed her up the staircase. "May I bring you some tea or scones?"

Aveline yawned. "That would be splendid." She considered herself lucky to have Godfrey and Miss Abernathy in her employ.

They were loyal to her family. Her father's coffers wouldn't pay them much longer, but the coin Miss McGuinness had given her would last until she acquired a suitor. Hopefully, that would not take more than six months.

County Tyrone, Ireland, 1824:

News travelled fast in County Tyrone. Everyone within a ten-mile radius soon knew that Seán O'Rooney resided in Dublin's Kilmainham Jail. The Court convicted him of attempted murder and dubbed him a thief. Before his arrest, many townspeople were victimized as debtors and thrown in a separate prison due to his money laundering. Riots raged in nearly every town demanding he be hanged.

Ciarán couldn't believe Solás and Eonán

had involved themselves in such an exciting adventure. He bid the men quit work for the day and they celebrated instead.

A crowd greeted them outside O'Malley's. A jovial group shouted in the streets.

MacRory ambled over to a few work-house acquaintances, while Ciarán's brothers talked amongst themselves.

Ciarán strolled in the direction of the bar. He grabbed a proffered pint and asked Molly in Gaelic. "What is going on here?"

She leaned over the wooden slab. "Did you hear about O'Rooney?"

He sipped. "Of course I did."

"We well know he's in Kilmainham, Blockhead, but there is more." She served a customer. "The constable found everyone's coin stashed in his cottage."

He drank half the glass. "Didn't know he lived anywhere other than the workhouse, all the better for the government's coffers."

"You forget who turned O'Rooney in." Molly smirked. "Since he stole from us, each *punt* will return to the owners' hands. The magistrate couldn't stand knowing two Irish citizens had captured the area's most wanted fugitive. It was the least they could offer."

He shook his head. "They'll raise taxes, you know, once they return the funds."

She laughed. "All the better for those with a full purse."

Ciarán finished his pint thinking about how much land he'd buy with two-thousand pounds.

👑 👑 👑

A month passed. The promissory notes were posted to Ciarán and he found himself at a Dublin land auction. He hadn't seen the city for years. The large pillared visage of Trinity College stood on his right. Rich memories of schooldays surrounded him.

MacRory had offered to watch the farm while he took the two-day trip. He admired the Scotsman's work ethic. The man enjoyed laboring.

A gentleman in a beaver hat stood on the street corner handing out hand bills. Ciarán approached and received one. The headline read, "Auction Today. Commences at two of the clock on College Green."

He smiled. He'd become a landowner in less than a half-hour. Hopefully, the property would be located in County Tyrone. Maybe he'd win a large plot outside Omagh.

The crowd surrounded a stone statue of Henry Grattan. The auctioneer stood on a couple of crates. He held a deed in the air, waving it haphazardly. A light wind rippled his clothing. "This me fine folks is a deed to thirty-plus acres outside Omagh. Pure farmland. Who'll start the bidding? Let's say fifty pounds." The man's English accent sounded strained.

Ciarán could do fifty, no problem. He raised his right hand.

The man in the beaver hat pointed. "Fifty to the man in the brown coat. Do we hear sixty?"

Each time the number escalated, Ciarán raised his hand. But when the price rose to five-hundred pounds, he stayed his hand. He couldn't empty a quarter of his purse on a family farm.

The speaker repeated the offer.

Then he heard a blonde-haired man mutter to a friend behind him. "Are you sure it's Altmore Farm?"

"Yes. The landowner put the lands up for sale a few days ago," a woman replied.

What the hell, he thought. Aveline was selling *his* farm? If he ever saw her again...

The man on the crates shouted. "Going once. Going twice—"

...he'd kiss her all over. Ciarán raised both hands.

"Sold! To the man in the brown coat. What is your name, sir?"

His brain thrummed. "O'Devlin. Ciarán O'Devlin."

"Congratulations, Mr. O'Devlin. You've bought yourself a farm."

Finally, he owned the bleeding property. He'd go into debtors' prison before the land fell into another's hands again.

Handing over the notes, he yanked the deed from the man. He hadn't read the contents since Lord Peyton showed him the deed many years ago. *I'm a landowner*, he thought. Folding the paper, he shoved it into his coat pocket. He needed another pint. Now.

👑 👑 👑

Every day after supper, ensconced in his bedchamber, Ciarán would read anything he could get his hands on.

Aveline hadn't returned. Although he'd prayed every night that she would. Days continued to come and go, and books allowed him to escape his thoughts long enough to focus on his work. He rather enjoyed reading, and the stories provided him enough distraction to relax.

Then he'd hear Aveline singing in his head, the way she had sung him to sleep every night.

'So soon may I follow when
friendships decay,
And from love's shining circle
the gems drop away.
When true hearts lie withered
and fond ones are flown.
Oh who would inhabit
this bleak world alone?'

County Cumbria, England, 1824:

For a whole month, Aveline was unable to sleep. She lay in bed each night with tears in her eyes and memories of the man who never returned her affections.

She looked down at her empty desk. Her dreams for publishing her first novel were now impossible. Her novel was in Ireland, and according to a letter from Mills Publishing, it would've taken more than fifty pounds, she could not expend, to accomplish the printing. Of course, if the book sold well, she'd receive more than what she paid in return.

Soon, the month of insomnia turned into many more.

She was lovesick. Well, sickness was the only explanation she could find for her condition. She couldn't eat much of anything, without feeling absolutely atrocious afterwards. The fact she was unable to last through each day without a nap wore heavily upon her. She'd spent every waking minute since her arrival in England focused on Ciarán. The man refused to leave her mind.

She imagined his arms wrapped around her as his lips touched hers. She'd taken his robe from Ireland and wore it every day, imagining his scent flooding her nostrils, even long after it had faded from the garment.

Aveline considered herself a besotted fool.

She was unsure whether she should resume her former contacts or not. They would notice her condition as soon as she sat down to tea. Still she longed for friends and wished to dance at soirees with handsome gentlemen, but it was much too late for that.

Her maid bustled into the room, noticing Aveline's reluctance to move from her desk. "What has you so down today, ma'm? Shall I fetch you a cup of chamomile tea before your nap?"

Aveline smiled wryly. "I am quite fine, Edith. I do not believe tea shall be necessary, although, I do appreciate your concern." She could not tell her maid she pined over a man who lived in Ireland. Only a weak soul allowed others to affect their lives like this.

Miss Abernathy looked down.

Aveline knew that Edith would never judge her, but she surely had noticed the weight gain and her increased fatigue. Without question, Aveline's dresses were altered at the waistline and she was given light meals in her bedchamber. She could not thank her maid enough.

"Please take care of yourself. I would not want you to suffer the same...I am not saying you..." The maid bit her lip.

Aveline did not wish to repeat the conversation. The woman worried herself to death over her pregnancy, but she could not take any more precautions. Yes, her mother had died from complications, but she did not believe she would. "I am well aware what my condition entails. I do not need any assistance into bed, Edith. I will call if I require anything else."

Miss Abernathy nodded and curtsied. The woman would retire to the bedchamber beside Aveline's and wait the whole day for her call.

Aveline didn't need another mother. All she desired was Ciarán.

The Irishman would make a fine husband. His perseverance and confidence were fine traits in a husband. But he didn't want to marry her.

Writing a letter to him would make everything feel worse. She couldn't bear another rejection. He already lived a complicated life and didn't need her added intrusion.

"By the Gods!" as her father would say, she loved him with all her heart.

Chapter 26

County Tyrone, Ireland, 1825:

Six months crept past before Ciarán visited Aveline's bedchamber. The winter crops were sold, and the soil well prepared for the spring. Seeing her empty room completely unraveled him. The sadness brought on a tearful remembrance of the woman who had walked away.

The loss of her presence addled Ciarán, but what he found in her room cauterized his bleeding heart as soon as his fingers closed on the papers. He held the book she wrote. Her smooth script covered over a hundred pages. The inkwell and pen lay on the small desk next to the stack. He blew off the thin dust veil covering the desk and paper.

The book's first page contained only the title, *Kissed By A Rose*.

On the second page, he found a small note with her signature attached.

To whom this book truly belongs,
I cannot say.
But to those who get the chance to read it,
I hope what you learn from its bindings,
Will carry with you through each day.
~ Aveline Maeve Peyton

Ciarán read the book, using it as her re-placement, allowing the memories of the time he shared with her to fill his mind. Each page contained her thoughts, and he was sure the words were written for him.

👑 👑 👑

Yes, he read the book even though she'd been gone a year. Alone with her words in the bedroom, time did not seem to matter, nor did the farm, really. He used his work as an excuse to earn wages for his brothers and MacRory, but lost all enjoyment in his previously-favorite pastime.

The book's pages flapped in a breeze that suddenly appeared in the room. A few candles on the bureau fluttered out.

From the corner of his eye, he saw *her* appear in the doorway. His daughter. Unafraid of anything to come since his future was already destitute, he spoke to her. "Hello, *mo iníon.*" He believed himself on the edge of madness, because he saw her curtsy in return to his words.

Ciarán stared at the little girl as she smiled. He knew if he walked over to her, he'd chase her away, but curiosity took hold of him. Intending to leave the room, anyhow, he rose from the worn leather chair.

With a slight giggle behind her tiny hand, she turned. He followed and watched as she ran down the stairs and disappeared.

Smoothing a hand down his face, he came back into the room and found a single red rose resting upon the quilt on the bed. He lifted the small stem and smelled its sweet fragrance.

Suddenly, he knew how to get Aveline back again.

♛ ♛ ♛

The next morning, Ciarán gathered all his money and met Afton in the field.

"I need you to watch the farm, MacRory. I'm leaving tomorrow."

The Scotsman did not offer any protest. "Tell the lass I wish her well."

He turned to his friend wide-eyed. "How

did you know me destination was England?"

Afton smirked. "A lucky guess, I s'pose. You mention the woman every day. 'Tis no wonder to me why you became a landowner."

Ciarán grinned. "You're right. MacRory, I know I've not always been the best leader. I remain aloof an' I give too many demmed orders." He wanted to make sense to someone for once.

Afton dropped the tools, clearly unaccustomed to Ciarán's current mood. "Are you sure you are up to the journey, O'Devlin?"

Why didn't Afton laugh instead? Ciarán sighed. He could not hold in the words. "I am quite all right. I just need to get something off me chest before we part. Thank you for being me friend all these years, Afton."

The Scotsman looked speechless.

"Tell me brothers, I will see them soon an' not to worry about me absence."

Afton nodded.

"Oh, an' one more thing. Yes, I am going to find Aveline. I am going to tell her she is the very air I breathe an' I cannot live without her. Then, I will ask her to marry me." Ciarán smiled. It felt wonderful to speak his mind. "Do you think she will say yes?"

Afton scratched his beard. "I suppose so, O'Devlin."

Ciarán smiled and put on his flat cap. "Grand. Have a good day, Afton."

He left the Scotsman grinning after him.

Chapter 27

County Cumbria, England, 1825:

Ciarán knew Aveline was born in Kendal, England, so he spent a whole day and night below decks on a scheduled ship called *Primrose* getting to England. The damp, dark steerage area was crowded with cargo and dirty, while rats scurried around him as their tiny feet pattered against the stiff floor. Without bedding, the wooden pole he leaned against dug hard into his backside. Not soon enough, he arrived on shore in a town called Ravenglass in Yorkshire. He walked with a straight back toward the captain who waited at the dock, greeting those who disembarked from the ship.

His greatest test approached—asking an Englishman for help.

He must've looked outright devilish to the gent, who gave him an unguarded smile, because Ciarán hadn't dedicated enough time to bring clean clothing. Nor a blade to rid the hair from his face.

He rubbed his stubbly jaw and spoke to the man in his clearest English. "Greetings, me good sir. Are you able to point me in the direction o' the town o' Kendal?"

The man glanced furtively at his worn black brogues. "Of course, but allow me to ask how you are to get there?"

The Englishman stared at his clothes as he asked. Ciarán figured he had probably never seen a man wear corduroy breeches, especially since they were not cut in the latest fashion. The English only respected those who wore the most fashionable clothing style. His dirty shirt was tucked in halfway. His coat had displayed a torn sleeve and a frayed hem. But then all the clothing he had ever owned was frayed or dusty.

"Public transport costs at least ten shillings," the sailor said. Maybe he deduced that Ciarán didn't have enough money for transportation if he was unable to buy nice clothes.

Ciarán nearly rolled his eyes. "I have the means to afford a passage. Between you and me, this is me first time upon these shores, an' I am in search o' a close friend."

The Englishman grinned mockingly and Ciarán's temper flared. "I've come a long way an' I am weary ta the bone. Where is the coach found that will take me?"

The man pointed toward the north. "Over

there. You do not want to be late. The coach does not come back for three hours."

Ciarán ran to stand with the people gathered near the road. The English chatter made his ears ring. Aveline didn't sound like any of them.

The stage coach came a half hour later, rolling up the path. Dust spread over whoever was in its wake. Ciarán sat next to an elderly couple who looked at him with sympathy. He did not glance toward them but stared out the window, overtaken by his thoughts.

How could he have been such a fool as to let Aveline go? She had given her heart to him, along with everything else she held dear. She hadn't come to Ireland to take his land. Instead, she had come on her father's orders. He had used her for his own carnal pleasures and hadn't thought about her feelings first or even his own honor.

He remembered the time he had believed

there wasn't an Englishman in existence with any feelings. Then he met her father. Lord Peyton wouldn't send his only daughter to denigrate Ciarán's earned place in Irish society. He could not hope for a greater friend and father figure than the late earl.

Since Aveline's departure, Ciarán couldn't wipe her memory from his mind. Instead he was traveling to the country he dreaded the most, determined to find her. Could this be her father's plan all along? Was it to unite them through these circumstances, despite their different cultures?

He noticed the countryside rushing past. The view was not so unlike his home, really.

The coach jolted to a stop a couple of hours later, telling him they had arrived at their destination. He waited his turn to exit. Stepping down onto the graveled road, he noticed a large manse in the distance, along with several smaller buildings surrounding it. Kendal was upon him. Walking toward the estate, he felt sure for the first time in his whole life.

Knocking upon the towering doors, he heard footsteps echo behind and then a butler opened them.

"I wish to see Lady Aveline," Ciarán said.

"Lady Aveline is not receiving today, sir, may I give her your card?" The butler looked him up and down dubiously before attempting to shut the door.

Ciarán responded by shoving it open wider.

The servant was wedged in between the door and the wall. "Sir, I do not know who you are, but you are most certainly not welcome in this house. The lady forbids me to open the doors to anyone. What makes you think you are someone she is willing to see?"

The Irishman leaned more heavily upon the entry. "Are you so sure o' the fact she does not wish to see me?"

Then he realized he was no longer in his own country, and that abusing people was the wrong way to go about getting what he desired.

The servant wailed, "Please, you must let me out at once!"

Ciarán was about to respond when he heard her voice.

👑 👑 👑

"Godfrey, what on Earth's name is causing all the noise? Surely, you must have a reasonable explanation for this clamor? You've nearly woken the...the..." Aveline's slippered foot hesitated above the bottom step on the staircase.

Ciarán looked upon her with adoration.

Even ragged and unkempt from traveling far and fast, he remained the same man she dreamt about every day for a whole year.

Aveline cradled a small bundle in her

arms. Her light blue gown with silver embroidery suddenly seemed thin and wanton, as did the hair curling down her back. She hungered for him. Even through the dirt and unkemptness, she saw the handsome Irishman she'd given her heart to. She wanted to run to him and throw her arms around his neck. She longed for the same soul-shattering embrace they had shared so many times before. She missed the farm and missed living in Ireland.

He didn't know about anything she'd gone through when she returned home—heartache, loneliness, to name just a few torments.

All those dreadful memories hurtled back into her mind upon seeing him and her hackles rose.

"My, my, Godfrey, what are we to do with him? Poor fellow he must be crazed to come prancing in here expecting me to show him any kindness." She did not dare move any closer. "Let my man out from there and mayhap we can talk a bit about certain things that have come to pass."

Ciarán immediately moved away from the door, shifting closer to her. She saw him look toward the bundle in her arms. Maybe he would believe she married someone else, that she had moved on from him so fast she'd landed a husband and a child.

His hands extended. "What is this, Aveline? I come to plead for me own forgiveness. I should not have done to you what I did." He sounded desperate, though appeared to be trying not to. "The time may be too late, but I want you to know you've never left me mind since you departed *Éire*."

Her heart fluttered. He still pulled at its strings. "What do you mean the time may be too late?"

Ciarán did not hesitate to answer. "You must've found someone else, surely. 'Tis the only explanation for—"

He gestured in the bundle's direction.

Aveline shook her head. "There is much you do not know, I can see. Let me enlighten you." She stepped onto the floor. "For the whole year we've been apart, I've not thought about anyone else. I did not truly plan on leaving Ireland. I wished for you to follow. I wanted to remain on the farm." She lowered her voice and he moved closer. "As I waited for the stage coach in Carrickmore, a man in a strange black carriage kidnapped me. I was bound, gagged and then thrown in-to the back." Tears formed in her eyes.

His eyes widened and the blood drained from his face. "I would've saved you if I'd known. How did you escape?"

"Poor clueless man. Your brothers, Eónan and Solás, apprehended O'Rooney, and Miss McGuinness freed me from my bonds. Alt-hough, I was free to return to the farm, the barmaid told me I should leave the country or O'Rooney would come after me. So I left."

Ciarán looked so forlorn. Maybe she should've written him, after all.

"Soon after I returned to England, I found I was with child. In order to make us a living, I sold the farm."

She would've become a servant otherwise, she thought as she looked down at the sleeping baby. "I am cradling your baby daughter, Ciarán. Her name is Éirinn."

The child's dark hair shown through the pink blanket. Her face twitched in sleep.

The English translation for their daughter's name was "peace." He was speechless. Aveline could see he battled strong emotions inside.

Her words had truly affected him, but she could not let the conversation end this way. "Do you think I should still forgive you now that you know the truth?" She noticed a change in him and it amused her. His Irish nature would not allow him to be silent on any subject, especially matters involving the heart.

Ciarán smoothed a hand over his face. "Right, you should not." He talked in a quiet undertone and a palm rested upon his heart. "I love you, *cailín dathúil,* an' although I have wronged you unmercifully, I hope you can have it in ya heart to forgive me for the mistakes I've made." His eyes met hers. "Never a day passed when I did not dream of you in me arms, when ya voice didn't fail to carry me off to slumber, an' when the very thought of you healed me tortured soul. I watched you walk away from me once, an' I will not stand for it to happen again, Aveline."

His feelings were spilling out with every word, and she relished each one.

"Ya father...um..." He paused.

Aveline could not tear her eyes away. She wished they were back in Ireland, back in the

Irish farmhouse, raising their daughter together.

She felt a single tear fall and spoke when he did not. "I have never stopped loving you since the first day we met. Please continue speaking. You know how much I enjoy hearing about my father."

His blue eyes shone brighter. "Ya father was a great man. Far greater than he taught me to become, obviously, because I did not see the world around me sooner."

Sadness swamped Aveline as she waved Godfrey out of the room. "*What* did he wish you to see, Ciarán?"

The manservant left with a last contemptuous look toward the Irishman. Ciarán didn't even notice. His eyes remained locked on hers.

She goaded him with a smile. "You did not explain to me what exactly my father wished from you, so please do continue with that subject."

A silence fell.

He removed his jacket and rolled up his sleeves. The same way he prepared for work on the farm. "Aveline, 'twas ya father who sent you to *Éire* to meet me."

She became defensive, as her Irish heat flowed through her veins.

"Nonsense—my father did no such thing. He would never force a courtship upon me. Whom I wished to marry was my choice. Besides, Papa surely knew we were never acquainted beforehand."

Ciarán scoffed. "Now you are makin' excuses for us. Suppose he thought an introduction wouldn't matter. Suppose he thought telling you what to do wouldn't have worked as you are as contrary as ever any mule. He did not know if we would get along. I'm saying his intentions for you were to marry me, because we would make a good match. He knew you could be happy with me, Aveline.

We'd own the farm together an' no longer live alone."

She could not believe it. "My father never spoke of me having to marry anyone. I daresay he personally disliked all the suitors for my hand. Do you think love would make me happy?" She walked another step toward him.

He moved ever closer. "You wrote about it in ya book."

Her voice grew husky. "So you read my book. Knowing that does not help your case in the least."

His dimpled smile returned. "You left the ribbon-wrapped papers in the farmhouse with a note, you did. What was I supposed to do when you left? I wanted to feel ya soul touch mine again. Ya story is unforgettable, Aveline."

Her resolve grew weaker. "I wrote the whole manuscript with your inspiration, but never you mind. It's no use pining over this nonsensical relationship any longer."

The longer she stood in his presence, the more she forgave him for all his misdeeds. She couldn't seem to remember why she was upset with him. She called for Edith to come fetch the sleeping Éirinn and take her to the nursery. She turned to Ciarán, who stood close enough to breathe upon her cheek, and fell into his arms.

"Will you marry me, Aveline?"

His words wrapped around her like a warm Irish breeze, the way his touch caused her to melt into his embrace.

She gasped. "Is it possible?"

"How do you mean?" he asked. "I bought me farm an' make good wages on it."

She pulled away, breathing heavily. "You did?"

Ciarán nodded.

She thought he'd—they'd—lose the Altmore Farm forever. Fate had led him to what he most desired.

"I will introduce you to Éirinn when she awakens, then we may discuss what is to come. For now, we must not talk."

He whispered musically in her ear. "Why ever not, *cailín dathúil*?"

"Well, for one thing, you need to visit a bath and dress yourself in fresh clothes," she jested with a smile. "I cannot be influenced to do anything with that foul smell lingering in my nostrils."

He chuckled. "Right, so you are saying you can be influenced to marry me, just not right this moment?"

She clung to his shirt, refusing to let him go a second time. "Yes—well—among other more exciting endeavors…"

Ciarán wrapped her face in his hands. "Would this help ya plight?" His head bowed until his mouth hovered over hers, then he kissed her softly upon the lips.

THE END

Author's Note

Thank you for reading the story of Ciarán and Aveline O'Devlin. The Irish culture has always intrigued me, being half-Irish, I find a lot of fun in researching the heritage. Truthfully, there is not much information pre-famine 1800s about Ireland's history. I suppose it is up to writers to make some magic of our own to create the story in between.

I used two songs throughout the novel that I believe correspond beautifully with the novel's basic themes:

"The Wearing of the Green" written by an anonymous author in 1798 and "The Last Rose of Summer" written by Thomas Moore in 1805. The melody to the song was later written by Sir John Stevenson between 1807 and 1834.

The poem used in Aveline's book *Kissed By A Rose* was written by me as was the note she left inside it for Ciarán.

About the Author

Diva Jefferson has a colorful relationship with the romance genre and has been writing for over 10 years. She is a member of the National Romance Writers of America, the Celtic Hearts Romance Writers, and the South Carolina Writer's Workshop.

www.ingramcontent.com/pod-product-compliance
Lightning Source LLC
Chambersburg PA
CBHW060512180626
46817CB00002B/356